Afternoon
of a
Good Woman

A *Consortium* BOOK

Afternoon
of a
Good Woman

Nina Bawden

HARPER & ROW, PUBLISHERS
New York, Hagerstown, San Francisco, London

ℒ. 5·30

ISBN: 0-06-010237-3

LIBRARY OF CONGRESS CATALOG CARD NUMBER: 76-26261

77 78 79 80 10 9 8 7 6 5 4 3 2

For
Juliet O'Hea and John Guest

Human law – what a farce!

TOLSTOY

For
Juliet O'Hea and John Guest

Human law – what a farce!

TOLSTOY

Part One

Today, Tuesday, the day that Penelope has chosen to leave her husband, is the first really warm day of spring. Her decision, last-minute but well researched, happens, through some chance (or perhaps characteristic) ineptitude, to coincide with her sitting, at ten o'clock in the morning, in judgement on her peers. She is a Justice of the Peace, a scrupulous woman, and the absurdity of this arrangement is evident to her — the errant suburban housewife posing as one of society's respectable pillars — but it is much too late to get out of it now. Petty sessional courts are required to provide magistrates to assist circuit judges at the Crown Court, and Penelope's place on the rota was fixed months ago. Although she could telephone the Clerk to say she has been taken ill suddenly, it seems wrong to start her new life with a lie. She is aware of the irony here; but life is full of small ironies, and at her age, which is forty-seven, she has learned to accept them. Indeed, this one comforts her as she takes a last look in her bedroom mirror (she is wearing her new blue velvet suit and is pleased to see how well it becomes her) before going downstairs to kiss Eddie goodbye. At least she is not leaving her husband, innocently washing the breakfast dishes in his sunny kitchen, to go straight to the arms of her lover.

Eddie's kiss tastes and smells of tobacco. He says, 'Have a good day, Penelope, darling,' and I feel a faint pang at the sound of my name. Penelope was such a faithful, long-suffering wife, wasn't she? But the guilt I begin to feel as I drive away (seeing my stay-

9

at-home Ulysses cheerily waving, dishcloth in hand, at the door)
is not because I am leaving him, nor because he doesn't yet know
it. Since I must go, this is much the best way. Eddie cannot bear
scenes. They make him weep; and, although most of his minor
failings – his drinking, his idleness, his boastful, arrogant driving
– no longer annoy me, his tears make me angry (they embarrass
me, I suppose), and I don't want to leave him in anger. I am too
fond of him – have felt, perversely, more genuinely loving towards
him these last few days than I have for a long time. Dear Eddie!
Poor Eddie – how will he manage? And so on, and so forth. I
have consoled myself with the thought that no one is indispensable
and he will be better off, once the first shock is over, without me.
As will the two girls. Like their father, they have leaned on me for
too long; like him, they are lazy. It is time they learned how to
arrange their own lives without always running to Mummy! (The
Liberation of Middle-aged Parents is a cause much closer to my
heart than Women's Lib., I sometimes jokingly tell them.) Though
no doubt their childish dependence will be a useful distraction for
Eddie in his new situation. Two great daughters to comfort and
care for will give him plenty to think about; provide him with a
rewarding, fatherly role to play that my more dominant presence
may, in the past, have denied him.

Even if these arguments are a bit specious, a bit hypocritical, I
honestly do not feel, at this moment, any real guilt about Eddie.
The nagging discomfort that invades me as I drive down the leafy,
suburban road this lovely spring morning has another cause
altogether. And a much odder one. Last week I received through
the post a brown envelope containing twenty loose aspirin tablets.
Nothing to say where they came from: my name and address
printed on the envelope in scarlet ink, in clumsy block capitals,
but no letter inside. As the postmark was local I assumed, to begin
with, that the sender must be some aggrieved, convicted defendant
in a case I had recently sat on. The message, though, seemed somewhat arcane. 'Hemlock is hard to get hold of, perhaps,' was Eddie's

suggestion and, although I laughed when he made it, I have been uneasy since. All this last week a growing disquiet has been my constant companion. Several nights I have woken up, my heart pounding with vague, formless fears. What frightened me, I slowly decided, was not so much *who* had sent me those tablets, but *why*. What was I supposed to have done? An explicit attack would have been much less disturbing. Lying awake, Eddie snoring thunderously by my side in the darkness, I found myself hoping another letter would come. Not because it might throw light on the first one (though I would have given this logical reason if asked), but because I felt, superstitiously, that if the event were repeated it would lose power in some semi-magical way. I set the alarm-clock half an hour early in order to be first downstairs, first to pick up the post from the mat. I wanted to spare my family worry. I also wanted to keep my shame private. There is always something shameful in an anonymous, undefined accusation – there is no smoke without fire, people say – and from the moment that letter arrived I have felt increasingly threatened. Even out of doors in broad daylight, walking our elderly dog on the common (poor old chap – *he* will miss me; no one else bothers with him), I have felt absurdly exposed, a marked woman; even this morning, safe inside the warm womb of the car, I am conscious of eyes, watching and jeering. But the commuters have already left for the City, for their offices and their banks and their Harley Street surgeries, and it is too early for their wives to be shopping. There is no one about at this time of the morning, no one to see me leaving my home for the last time, leaving my husband and daughters. . . .

Open white gates and a fine, spreading cedar, pale-tipped with new growth, mark the end of our road; the exit and entrance to the private housing-estate of Cedar Grove. My daughters call it 'Funny Farm Wood' because it is built round the old mental asylum. This towered and turreted Gothic extravagance (the charitable gift to the nation of an eccentric patent-medicine millionaire) is still in use as a hospital for psychiatric patients, but its landscaped grounds were sold in the thirties and are now covered with comfortable, prosperous houses, each secluded behind high hedges and concealing shrubberies. Rhododendrons grow well in this soil and are in flower now; heavy blossoms against stiff, polished foliage.

Through the white gates I turn left past the village. Neat, bright-gardened cottages cluster round a wide green with a pond and a public house carefully restored to rustic antiquity. On one side of the green the main tower of the asylum rears up on the skyline, balancing, in its bizarre fantasy, the weird moonscape of the motorway that is being built on the other. Both are lunatic invaders in this gentle valley, ridiculously out of scale with the small fields, the little hills, the pretty toy village; but the road, being new, is the obvious enemy. For some, anyway. Local industry needs the road. It is the rich residents of Cedar Grove who have fought against it, and their class-based hostility seems to me greedy and ugly. Men's jobs – in the gravel pits, in the plastics factory – are more important than their lovely view! I am afraid I put this point of view rather forcefully to my indignant neighbours when they came to ask for my signature to one of their selfish petitions. Did one of them, perhaps, send me those aspirins? Meaning what? 'You God-awful prig, you give me a pain'? Or 'Finish yourself off, why don't you?'

Bumping carefully over a ramp, a damaged stretch of road under the soaring arch of the motorway, I feel my stomach muscles contract. I gave a loud, stupid laugh (as if to cover up an involuntary, public fart) and say, 'Ho, hum. No. Oh, no. Really!' It is too crude a thought. No one I know would go in for such a crude bit of spite. Eddie is right. Malicious chance aside, the most likely thing is some small local villain, a loutish boy I have fined or sent to an attendance centre, getting a bit of his own back. Seeing it as a bit of a giggle! And it is a more harmless protest than having your car tyres let down, or a brick heaved through

your drawing-room window! Certainly Eddie would have said so if I had let him know how deeply upset I was. 'A very minor hazard of being a respected mouthpiece of justice, my old duckie-doo.' Several times I have longed to hear his gravelly, chain smoker's voice say something like this, see his small, pale, almost lashless eyes blink with concern. Even one of the dotty endearments he uses (once out of shyness, now simply from worn, married habit) would have comforted me. But it hardly seemed fair in the circumstances, when I was on my way *out*, so to speak, to lumber him with my silly worries.

Why *am* I so upset? Transferred guilt about Eddie? Something in that, perhaps, but it is not the whole answer. Perverse pride comes into it. I enjoy my judicial function, the sense of power and position it gives me; but at the same time I want to be seen as a merciful woman, tempering the wind to the shorn lambs who appear before me. A kind of Lady Compassion, loved by her victims! No difference, I like to tell myself, between them and me except a small shift of luck. Persuading myself that I often see in their faces (the faces of the defeated, the inadequate, the unlucky, the lost) my own face reflected; hear, in their stumbling attempts at some mitigation of their small crimes, an echo of my own voice. And indeed, to be fair to myself (and, if I can't be fair to myself, how can I be trusted to be fair to others?), in the magistrate's court, where I sit almost weekly, the margin of error that puts me on the side of the judges and not of the judged sometimes seems very narrow.

Shoplifters, for example. Women my age steal from super-markets assorted ragbags of articles. Three packets mixed nuts, two tins scouring powder, a bottle of lemonade, black boot-polish, a pound of beef sausages, a dozen light-bulbs, a pair of nylon tights not their size. Caught, they say much the same things. They 'can't remember what happened'. They 'don't know what came over them'. They usually have enough money on them in their

worn purses, are willing – eager – to pay. They have recently
suffered from depression/the menopause/some domestic unhappiness. Husbands, taking the day off work, speak on their behalf
with lined, concerned faces. They have been married twenty/
twenty-five/thirty years. Have two/three/five children. Nothing
like this has ever happened before. The wife often weeps at this
point, the court usher takes her a glass of water and the magistrates
look away while she drinks it: her situation, so unbelievably
terrible to her, is embarrassingly common to them. Only rarely
does some small thing make a case of this kind memorable, turn
the court-room into a theatre. A husband stumbles as he speaks
of a family tragedy. Defending counsel leads gently. 'I believe
one of your children was ill at the time this incident happened?'
The husband weeps; old, shaking, veined hands clutching the edge
of the witness-box. 'Our son is dead now.'

Empathy, easy enough in a case of this kind, is harder in others.
Even as tears mist my vision, remembering that sad, humbled pair
(their physical appearance still clear in my mind's eye: her pallor
and crumpled cheeks, his bruised look of defeat), I recognise that
I cannot imagine myself throwing a bomb or beating up some
poor, defenceless old queer on the common. My heart does not
bleed for savages, nor for professional criminals. Thugs and
thieves are not social victims to me, still less social heroes.
Burglary is a job in which the rewards, though irregular, are often
better than an honest occupation; the hazards known and accepted.
  As falling foul of the law is often accepted, too, by the poor.
You can't pay your rates, the television licence, the tax on your
car, your ex-wife's maintenance. You land up in court and they
fine you and you can't pay the fine. This situation is not without
dignity, and some are aware of it. On the dual carriageway
(illegally speeding towards the Crown Court) I shoot past a
lumbering truck and think of a young lorry-driver whose handsome looks and good-natured expression went a long way to

explain the fix he found himself in. He had recently married for the third time. His new wife had just given birth to twin boys. Her retired father and crippled sister lived with them, and although they both had small pensions the lorry-driver's wages were swallowed up by rent and other household expenses. Unfortunately, he was supposed to be supporting, on several court orders, his two previous wives and their children. The arrears, predictably, were enormous. Asked by our chairman (a kind, elderly lady and noted soft touch) if he could possible manage to pay some of them, he smiled with a lovely, warm, amused tolerance. And instead of calling her Your Worship or Madam he said merrily, 'No, m'dear, bless you!' which along with the smile, she said afterwards, set up a pleasant flutter in her grandmotherly breast.

Few people, appearing in court, behave so agreeably. Reactions vary from the timid and terrified to the boldly defiant. Some motorists (noticing my speedometer flickering in the high seventies, I ease my foot on the accelerator) are frankly outraged. Company directors, caught belting along in their Rolls or their Bentley, put on superior smiles, exaggerate the drawling gentility of their voices, make subtle appeals to the magistrates as social equals. Absurd that people like us should be here at all, called to account in this humiliating way! As if we were criminals! Motoring offences are not really *crimes* – we all know that, don't we?

An unattractive attitude. Understandable, though, if you put yourself in the place of these solid citizens, used to judging their own behaviour, totting up their own deeds, good or bad, acquitting or convicting themselves. A court of law not only sharpens up, illuminates this everyday, private process, but also takes it out of their hands. And this is, in some way, defiling. To accuse yourself, even harshly, is one thing; to be accused quite another. Even if only by an anonymous letter, a handful of aspirins.

Was that, after all, such a crude accusation? I feel a shock of coldness like an icepack applied to the back of my neck, the nerves at the base of my skull. I give my loud, awkward laugh again –

'Ho, *hum*' – as it comes to me, suddenly, that it could have been a subtle, informed one. From someone with a long memory; someone who knew about Eve. . . .

Eve was – is – my stepmother. I have loved and welcomed her from the beginning – never resented her, as popular psychology might suppose. Although I did not miss my own mother (never having known her, how could I?), I missed the idea of her, if only in a conventional way. My father had stretched his income as a clerk in the Civil Service to send me to a small private school riddled with all the classic suburban snobberies, and I longed to be like all the other little girls and have a pretty, lady-like mother to meet me. No doubt I had deeper longings as well, but I cannot recall them; the most painful feeling I can remember is the shame I felt when I had to tell someone my mother was dead.

The string of 'aunties' my father provided to care for me while he worked were inadequate substitutes. Not just because they were busy housewives with their own children and readier, on the whole, with slaps than with kisses, but also because their common, working-class voices embarrassed me. I was often terrified when one of them came to fetch me from school that my friends or my teachers would mistake her for a relation. This fear made me rude. I would cry, 'Oh, there you are!' in a loud haughty voice, refusing to call the poor woman 'Auntie' or take her hand until we were out of sight of the building. Once we were alone, I would try to make up for this unendearing behaviour with smiles and sweetness, but though none of these women was ever unkind they were seldom affectionate. 'Be a good girl' was usually the parting injunction, once I was thought old enough to be left alone after tea. 'Don't play with the fire and don't worry your daddy.' I tried to be good and I don't think my father ever knew I was lonely. He had been brought up in an orphanage and probably thought that to have one parent was riches.

Eve's refined accent delighted me. Her first husband (who had knocked her about and whom she had fled from to marry my father) was a solicitor, a social position that seemed to me very elevated. I was ten when my father brought her home, and I adored her from the moment she opened her mouth. That she was pretty and kind and did not seem to despise our small, shabby house as I had feared she might was a wonderful bonus. I fawned round her feet like a puppy and would have been overjoyed to run errands for her and help with the cooking and cleaning, even if my father had not prompted me to. Eve, he told me, was 'not very strong'.

In what way, how or why, was not specified. She was very small and looked fragile as a piece of fine china. Even my little hands were bigger than hers and, feeling her fingers with delicate awe, I assumed that this was what Father meant. Eve was so frail she might break if you handled her roughly. She never spoke of what she had suffered at the hands of her brutal solicitor husband, but I thought of it often, with horror, and prayed that she would be happy with me and my kind, gentle father. 'Look after Eve, darling,' he said when he left to go overseas with the Army two years after they married, the third year of the war, and I assumed the charge proudly.

I was happy to be alone with Eve. I thought she was happy too, sharing my tea by the fire and playing whist when my homework was finished. The only bad times, for me, were when letters came from her children; from her son Steve or, worse still, from her younger child April, who was exactly my age. They were at boarding-school and spent most of their holidays with their father's family, but I was terrified that April would write one day and say she was miserable and wanted to live with her mother as she had done, very briefly, when Eve first married Father. She had shared my bedroom, and I had hated her. When Eve had come in to kiss us goodnight and bent over April's bed, lingering perhaps a second longer than she had over mine, I had felt such rage and anguish that it was all I could do not to cry out with the pain. I still felt bitterly jealous the mornings her letters came, even though Eve never read them while I was there, but I tried not to show it and always asked later on if April had said anything interesting. Though it hurt me to think it, Eve was probably fond of her daughter, and I did not want to hurt Eve. I wanted to love and protect her.

When she first became ill, I enjoyed looking after her. If I came home from school to find her still in her nightdress, sitting limply before the empty grate, or weeping into a stack of dirty dishes in the kitchen, I lit the fire, washed the dishes, made supper for us both. If there was nothing to eat in the house, I took Eve's purse and ran to the corner shop; later on, when it seemed that Eve was feeling too tired to go out at all, I took charge of the ration-books and began to shop regularly, on the way to and from school. I felt strong and competent, looking after my poor little stepmother, and though I hoped she would be better soon, for her own sake, I was glad to have been given this chance to show what I could do for her. Perhaps, when she recovered, Eve would write to Father and say what a help I had been these last weeks! More helpful than April would ever have been; that lazy girl, that great, idle lump!

One autumn evening I had a netball practice and came home later than usual. There were no lights on in the house. Eve was sitting in the dark kitchen, on the floor, under the table, crouched up and moaning. I drew the blackout curtains, put the lights on, brewed a pot of tea and asked her why she was crying. 'It's no use. I'm no use. I've done my best to be a good mother to you, sent my own babies away; but I can't do it. I can't look after you. What use am I?' She wailed as she said this, rocking from side to side, pretty, pale face puffy with misery, tears and cigarette-ash showering down. I thought it was strange that she should speak of Steve and April as babies. I said, 'You don't have to look after me, darling. I can look after *you*. Go to bed and have a nice rest. I'll clean up the kitchen and everything. Shall I get you a hot-water bottle?'

Eve smiled rather wildly. It seemed to split her face open. 'I have such a pain. In my head and my back. Like a burning rod down my spine.'

'Perhaps you ought to lie flat.'

I wondered if I should call the doctor. But the house looked so dreadful, dust everywhere, and Eve herself was so *dirty*: I saw, for the first time, the grey tidemark on her frail neck, her black fingernails. She looked so strange too, smiling and smiling in that wild, stupid way. She would hate the doctor to see her like that! I said, 'You'll be all right once you're tucked up in bed. I'll bring you a couple of aspirins and a hot-water bottle and make you some supper.'

I helped her upstairs, and she seemed better in bed, lying still and not crying, only occasionally letting out a long, sad, fluttering sigh. Next morning I got up early, cleaned the kitchen and the hall and the stairs in case the doctor had to be fetched after all, and took Eve her breakfast. 'I've got to go to school now but I'll come home dinner-time and get you some hot soup or something. You'll be all right, won't you?'

Eve smiled and smiled. She was like a stiff, smiling doll propped up on the pillows. I lit the gas-fire to make the room cosy for her and left the bottle of aspirins where she could reach it if the pain started up again. I was pleased by the efficient way I had organised everything and planned to give her a tin of tomato soup at midday. She ate so little (when I had helped her to bed she felt like a bird in my arms, all bones and no flesh) but she might take a little soup with some cheese grated into it.

After morning school I ran home like the wind. But, when I opened the front door and stumped, breathing hard, up the stairs, Eve was gone. One of our neighbours, a stout, red-faced woman in a flowered apron, stood in the doorway of her bedroom. She said, 'She's gone to hospital, Penelope, love. Don't be frightened,' and closed the door quickly as if there was something inside she didn't want me to see.

While I stared, she talked quickly. We must get busy, she said, and pack up my clothes. She had already telephoned the people who were to look after me while Eve was in hospital – old friends of my father's who lived in the Midlands. I asked what was wrong with Eve, and she said, 'She was just taken poorly, dear, nothing to worry about; but hospital's the best place the way she's been feeling.' She took me home to her house and made a great fuss of me. Steve arrived late that afternoon while we were eating sardines on toast in the kitchen. The first thing he said to me was 'Why didn't you tell someone she wasn't well? Why did you leave her?' but the neighbour shook her head at him, pursing her mouth up, and he sighed, making a gritty sound with his teeth as if he had sand caught between them.

I said, 'I looked after her for ages and ages. I cleaned the house, and I washed all the dishes, even the saucepans, *and* I did all my homework.'

The woman said, 'It's been going on a long time by the looks of it. I've popped in once or twice, but you don't like to interfere, do you? Penelope's been very good. Done her best. You couldn't expect a child to do more.'

Steve nodded, still making that gritty sound with his teeth, standing awkwardly to attention between the kitchen stove and the table, big hands dangling out of his braided school blazer, beaky nose sweating, soft, boyish mouth trembling. He was just eighteen and bewildered by this man's role thrust upon him but anxious to perform well. He said finally, 'No, of course not. I'm sorry,' but though he smiled at me then very sweetly, I felt he still blamed me.

As I blame myself now. Do I? Do I *really*? No, of course not; that is pure affectation. A self-pitying luxury. I was twelve years old. How could I have known poor Eve was ill in that way, still less guessed that she might try to end it all, swallowing aspirins? Oh, I understand how Steve felt! What a nightmare for him. Presumably the neighbour had not known who else to get hold of.

Indeed, there *was* no one else: Eve had broken with her family when she married my father, and he had no parents living, no brothers, no sister.

No one else who could have known what had happened, let alone cared enough to have held it against me and sent me, nearly forty years later, that wicked reminder. That Steve should do such a thing is unthinkable! Too ridiculous. *I* am being ridiculous! I say so aloud as I park my car outside the Crown Court and sit for a moment, after I have switched off the engine, staring at the martial lines of pink tulips on parade in the flower-bed beyond the front bumper. 'Pull yourself together, Penelope; you are being bloody ridiculous!' Such a minor, if creepily unpleasant, incident. Why waste time and emotional energy trying to seek out the reason behind it? Particularly if all I can dredge up is something so remote as to be merely fanciful. My conscience has made the connection, of course. That busy organ is always beavering away fairly pointlessly, and on this occasion does not deserve to be listened to. Or only in one ear to be kicked promptly out through the other! I know perfectly well that I never meant to hurt Eve; that I had not even been distantly negligent, leaving a bottle of aspirins at her bedside, since I had not understood the state she was in. The defence of *mens rea,* I think, as I walk briskly up the steps of the court, smiling charmingly at the car-park attendant who opens the door for me. Guilt, to be proved, must be established in the mind.

As it will have to be in the main trial set down for today. Although the defendant has disposed of an old car that did not belong to him, selling it for five pounds to a breaker's yard, the circumstances were such that he might easily have assumed the wreck was abandoned. And, whatever the facts (stolen cars, aspirin bottles left within a mad woman's reach), if you had no guilty intention you cannot be guilty in law.

There is no significance in this small coincidence – or only the kind of significance people impose, reading their horoscopes in the morning newspaper at the end of the day and picking out the accurate forecasts. But I like to see life fall into patterns – that mysterious process the Italians call *sistemazione* – and even if, on this occasion, the artistic tidiness is only in my own mind it sharpens my interest in this simple case and gives me a feeling of kinship with the young man in the dock.

Abel Binder is a tractor-driver by trade; twenty-nine years old, a married man with two children, living with his wife's parents. His hobby is old motor cars. He doesn't own one himself, driving to and from the farm where he works on a Honda; but he does repairs for friends, working most evenings at a yard owned by the local council where he rents a garage. He makes a small charge but it seems he works mainly for pleasure, enjoying the exercise of a skill he has taught himself, taking pride in keeping machines on the road that most garages would consign to a scrap-heap. A decent, patient, rather slow young man, always willing to lend a hand. A bit too willing, perhaps. As the prosecution witnesses tell their various tales in the course of the morning, he begins to appear an innocent victim of chance. . . .

When last August (eight months ago now) a student turned up at the yard driving a battered Mercedes and towing another, a wreck written off in a crash, Abel offered to help him strip it down for salvage. But, although the student came to the yard several nights a week and discussed with Abel how best to 'cannibalise' the old car, he did nothing about it and went back to Oxford at the end of the summer vacation, leaving the car in one of the garages.

He had not told Abel he was at university. Cross-examined by Abel's counsel, he smiles. Mr Binder had not asked what he did; why should he have told him? They had only talked about cars – nothing else. It seems to me, at this point, that the student's smile is a bit patronising. A hint of *noblesse oblige*. This condescending young lordling would naturally adjust his conversation to his company! He wears tight-fitting jeans and a matching denim jacket with a black turtle-neck sweater; Abel a stiffly cut dark suit, white shirt and black tie.

At the beginning of December, a couple came to the yard when Abel was there. New to the district, they had applied to the Council and been allotted one of the garages: No. 9 at the end of the row. The key they had been sent fitted the padlock, but the student's old car was inside. 'I think it's been dumped,' Abel said.

The couple telephoned the Council and were told the garage ought to be empty. In fact (this bureaucratic muddle was not discovered till later) the garages had been renumbered in the office but not on the site. The husband returned to the yard in some indignation. Abel was sympathetic but it wasn't his business. He said, 'If anyone comes along from the Council, I'll see they do something about it.'

Several days passed. Abel invited a scrap-dealer to call at the yard. He had just finished a job and had some stuff to get rid of. When the man came, Abel said he was sorry but he had nothing for him. A gang of young hooligans had raided the yard overnight and 'cleaned the place up'. No, he had not told the police. What would the point be? He had lost a few old tyres, a couple of rusty bumpers. But the boys had smashed the padlock of No. 9 garage. 'What's that bit of junk, then?' the scrap-dealer asked. 'Just an old wreck that's been dumped,' Abel said. 'Worth a fiver to you?' He helped the man drag it out of the garage and fastened the tow-rope.

The university term ended. The student came to the yard and said, 'Where's my car?' When Abel answered, 'I don't know; I've not seen it,' he went to the police.

And Abel continued to lie. To the sergeant who called at his home and to the inspector who questioned him when he was arrested and taken to the police station. Not changing his story until they traced the scrap-dealer and the student identified what was left of his old Mercedes. Then Abel said, 'Oh, all right, then. I just didn't want trouble.'

At the close of the prosecution case, the Judge turns to me and says, 'This has gone on long enough, don't you think? Shall I suggest to the jury that they throw it out now?'

I nod and smile. I feel immensely relieved. It is so clear to me that Abel Binder is innocent, but in the eight years I have been a magistrate I have only sat six times at the Crown Court and this is the first time I have sat on a full trial with a jury. The procedure is slower and lengthier than I am used to in my own petty sessions; and I have been afraid, once or twice, that I may betray my impatience. Or, worse, that I may be too nervous, in this unfamiliar situation, to speak up when I should. I am grateful that I don't have to; that this judge is too sensible to allow a miscarriage of justice. He has intelligent, brown eyes with clear whites, and his breath smells of toast – not unpleasantly. I think: Perhaps he had no time to clean his teeth after breakfast; and sit back, composed and relaxed in my chair while he addresses the jury.

They are (he kindly informs them) men and women of the world and know what is meant by stealing. The legal definition, which he is bound to give them, is unlikely to conflict with their own common sense. According to the Theft Act, stealing means dishonestly appropriating goods belonging to another person, and the key word is *dishonestly*. The jury are entitled to hear the defence – indeed, if they have any doubts it is their duty to do so – but, if they have heard enough already to satisfy them that Abel Binder acted quite innocently, they can acquit him now. They must consider the evidence, using the worldly common sense he has mentioned, and remembering that the real question is whether the defendant had known he was in the wrong at the time he got rid of the car – not later, when the student turned up to claim it. This isn't hair-splitting but the crux of the matter. Although the jury may take into account the fact that Mr Binder lied to the police when judging his character, he is on trial for stealing, not lying.

Apart from one woman who has fallen asleep, plump chin on fur collar, the jury listen attentively to the Judge's instruction like good children in class. When he has finished some of them frown as if the intrusion of what seems a subjective moral assessment into this court of law is somehow improper. How are they to know what had gone on in Abel Binder's mind? Or perhaps they are simply confused. One elderly man is cupping a blue, knuckly hand at the back of his ear, although he has not appeared deaf before. It is confusing, of course, that innocence should emerge in the course of prosecution evidence. Incongruous, anyway.

Even Abel Binder looks puzzled, though perhaps that is natural. The lumbering process of law must often seem puzzling to the defendant: he knows the truth, after all! I look at Abel Binder, at his rocky, rosy, countryman's face. He looks disarmingly honest to me, but that is not evidence. People's faces – frowns, wrinkles, arched brows, lip-twitches, lowered lids, decorous or open smiles, thready webs of blood vessels – are an inadequate map for the enquiring voyager in the country of their minds. Clues to what goes on there are usually tangential: rational thought rarely discovers them. You can only interpret what you see and hear, sieve it through the mesh of your own impulses, desires, memories.

In court this natural process is rarely admitted. There is fact, evidence sworn to by witnesses holding the Testament few of them ever read, putting on suitably dignified masks for this solemn occasion. Question and answer is supposed to dredge the fine sand of truth from the mud of experience. It is not the business of judges to put themselves in the defendant's place, still less to use their own lives to embroider the facts of his as they know them. Not what you're here for, my girl, I tell myself when I catch myself doing it. Just pure self-indulgence. . . .

Abel is looking at me. I lift my chin and turn my head to the angle at which I know I look best, the violin curve of my cheek balancing my rather long, bony jaw. I am not ashamed of this little vanity. It is no sin to admit I am pleasant to look at! I smile at Abel, with discreet reassurance, and am slightly discomforted when he smiles back at me openly. Then think: Why on earth shouldn't we smile at each other? There is always a dialogue between the Bench and the dock: we are each providing a part for the other to play. So why not acknowledge it, exchange a human look? We may be enemies, but we are also conspirators. I am in a stronger position than Abel just at this moment, but I understand him, believe he is innocent, know why he told all those lies. It is a painfully familiar predicament. After one foolish blunder, the next is inevitable. You go on, covering up, because there is no alternative. . . .

The policeman said, 'Can you tell me what this man looked like, Penelope? Can you remember what he was wearing?' His smile was grave but gently encouraging. A family man with young daughters himself, he understood my embarrassment and would have spared me if he could, but other children must be protected. He said, 'Anything at all you can remember about him?'

I thought he seemed kind. It crossed my mind briefly that if we had been alone I might have told him the truth, thrown myself on his mercy. But Uncle and Auntie were sitting there, watching me. I looked at their red, solemn faces and then at Uncle's tweed hat and old gardening-coat hanging on the back of the kitchen door. I said, 'I think he was wearing a raincoat. A bit old and muddy. And a speckly hat. The sort of clothes men put on to go and dig in the garden.'

This was three days after my thirteenth birthday. I had been living with these friends of my father's whom I called 'Uncle' and 'Auntie' for more than six months, ever since Eve had been taken to hospital. They were a middle-aged couple (old, to my eyes) with grown children: two sons in the Forces, and a daughter married to an American banker who lived in New York and sent frequent food-parcels. I imagine the food-parcels were one of the reasons

Eve had chosen them to look after me – whispering their name and telephone to our neighbour as she was carried, retching and choking, into the ambulance. In the way of people who know they have failed in some important particular, she was trying to make amends in a minor way. This was one wartime household where she could be certain I would be properly fed!

I had never in my life eaten such regular and copious meals, and for a while this physical pleasure obscured the fact that neither Uncle nor Auntie had much else to offer. Uncle had been my father's boss when he first joined the Civil Service. He and Auntie had 'taken an interest', he told me, in 'the young, orphan boy', and I suppose my father was grateful. I can think of no other explanation for the friendship he felt for this greedy, stupid, portly pair. Women still wore corsets then, and Auntie was solidly armoured: a large, firm woman with a soft, florid face, a protruding lower lip, and a confident air that suggested she had once been a beauty. Early photographs lining the flock-papered walls of her sitting-room confirmed this impression; showed her romantically rising, sultry-eyed and bare-shouldered, from an artful background of mist.

In spite of these provocative pictures on public display, Auntie was a prurient woman. The day I arrived she came to my room while I was unpacking my suitcase and asked if I had started my periods. When I nodded, she lowered her voice to a whisper. 'Well, dear, if you have anything to burn, put it into the boiler when Uncle isn't around. Make sure of that, won't you?' The colour rose in her cheeks as she added, with a mysterious air of self-congratulation, 'You see, Penelope, Uncle and I have never discussed that sort of thing, not in our whole married life.'

This odd request puzzled me to begin with; later it became an embarrassment. I was anxious to comply with the customs that prevailed in this household (where would I go if I didn't?) but, as it turned out, there were tactical difficulties. Uncle had retired from the Civil Service and, although he was 'helping out' in the local offices as his contribution to the war effort, he worked irregular hours. The main rooms of the house were seldom used, to save fuel, and when I was there he was usually in the kitchen, sitting in his wheelback chair by the boiler reading the paper, or pottering in the adjacent scullery where he had a handyman's bench. And, even if he was out at a time I was in, I was afraid he might open the front door and meet me coming downstairs or crossing the hall. For several months I avoided the issue by wrapping my sanitary towels in old newspaper and hiding them in a drawer beneath my school underwear. The drawer began to smell after a while, and I was afraid Auntie would notice. The absurdity of the situation was clear to me, but I could not see what to do about it: an irrational sense of guilt had so supplanted all reason that even when I was alone in the house I did not dare carry the rubbish downstairs and burn it. There was too much of it now, anyway! Stuffed into the boiler, it would stink to high heaven! It might even put out the fire, and it was Uncle's job to rake out the ashes.

I took a few of the towels to school in my satchel and put them in the bins in the lavatories. But they made my books smell, and my satchel, and after a while I began to feel that a stale, vegetable odour surrounded me, clung to my hair, to my clothes. The other girls must be aware of it! I kept aloof from them, in the classroom, in the playground. Lonely anyway, being new to the school, I grew lonelier.

The quickest way from the house to the school, the short cut, led through the town cemetery. It was winter, and after some days of harsh winds and heavy skies the snow fell. Soft balls of white fuzz, falling and falling and covering the cold earth with a concealing blanket. One evening, Auntie and Uncle were out playing bridge. I packed up a newspaper parcel and ran to the cemetery. Snow was mounded thick over the sleeping graves. I read the inscription on the tombstone as I buried my parcel, and hoped that Annie Ramsbottom, whose menstrual problems were over now she was safe in the arms of Jesus, would look down and forgive me.

For some days I was demented with joy. I sang round the house, asked if I might bring a friend home to tea, chattered and laughed. Auntie and Uncle seemed to respond with relief to this change in me. They both said several times that they were glad I was 'settling in'. 'I think the ice has broken at last, hasn't it?' Uncle said one evening when we were alone in the kitchen. He put his arm round me and fondled my breast with hard, probing fingers, but this clumsy assault alarmed me less than his arch remark. It had a frighteningly prophetic ring.

And, of course, the thaw started. Dangling icicles dripped from the gutters; starved, yellow grass appeared in the gardens. A brisk wind got up, increasing one morning to almost gale force. Waking to the slap and thump in the chimney, I lay in my narrow bed hypnotised by a horrible vision. My newspaper parcel disintegrating; my bloody towels blowing all over the cemetery.

No one would know they belonged to me. All the same, I felt a numb terror of a kind I had not known since I was very small and believed God could see me whatever I did: that even if I locked the door of the lavatory his eyes might appear in the ceiling like two huge, glaring light-bulbs! I didn't believe in God anymore (when I prayed, it was only for form's sake), but the fear of some sinister, all-seeing authority returned and possessed me. I went the long way to school, through the town, arriving too late for morning assembly. After a week, my form mistress took me aside. Not to reprove me but to make a kindly enquiry. She knew my situation. She asked if everything was 'all right' where I was staying. It could be difficult, sometimes, living with strangers. I mumbled that I was very happy; but she persisted, taking my hand and saying that I must try to look on her as a friend and speak honestly. Was I sure there was nothing wrong? She had thought I looked worried lately. There must be some reason why I was late every morning. I looked into her sweet, concerned face and said hoarsely, 'I have to wash the breakfast dishes before I leave. It makes me late. I can't help it.'

Since I knew I was lying, I didn't expect her to believe me and when she appeared to, felt deeply depressed. Perhaps I had half-hoped the truth would come out in some painless way and I would be forgiven. But I was only depressed, not afraid. It didn't occur to me that my kind teacher would feel it her duty to approach Uncle and Auntie.

Auntie said, one day at tea, 'I don't understand why you should be late for school. You leave in plenty of time, don't you?'

Her tone was withdrawn. She wouldn't accuse me directly, even though the school's suggestion that she was using me as a domestic servant must have outraged and shamed her. I knew this, and was sorry, but couldn't see how to repair the damage. I muttered, 'Only if I go through the cemetery. I don't like to. Not now.'

My face burned. I stared at the floor. Eventually Auntie said, 'Of course it can be lonely sometimes during the winter. Especially for a girl, these dark mornings.' She sounded more excited than angry. Looking up, I saw her eyes glitter. She said, 'You must tell me, Penelope. Has anything – *anyone* – upset you?'

I understood her at once. There was only one subject that made her eyes shine like that! I nodded, biting my lip, and was instantly clasped to her large, bolstered bosom. Her voice sang with lyrical tenderness. 'My poor child, why didn't you tell me? Were you afraid to? Oh, of course, you would be! But it's all over now. darling. You don't even have to tell me about it if you really don't want to.'

But I did have to tell her, of course. Was trapped, by that first lie, into a labyrinth of falsehood, all exits cut off. Snared, silly bird, into a net that tightened lubriciously round me as Uncle was told the harrowing tale, the police called. . . .

We sat in the kitchen, Uncle and Auntie, the policeman and I. The boiler crackled and hissed. I looked at Uncle, put a hand to my breast; then, when he looked away, said to the policeman, 'He

didn't touch me but he had his John Thomas out and told me to look. And he had mad sort of eyes, bright like torches.'

I have only once seen a rapist, brought before our bench to be committed for trial at a higher court. An animal, wild-eyed through matted hair. Flashers (as men who expose themselves are commonly called) are rarely so exotic. Shambling failures, immature adolescents, lonely old men – in the dock they appear either helpless or hopeless or so devastatingly respectable that it is hard to comprehend the sad, shuddering need that has brought them there. Or the excited emotion they arouse in their victims. Some women invite their behaviour. One makes a complaint to the police: standing at the window of her sitting-room one autumn afternoon, she has seen the Italian gardener working next door unzip and masturbate in the gap of the hedge. Maybe he did, but why was she watching? The defence produces measurements: these are large gardens; the woman could only have seen what the man was up to if she had been looking through a pair of binoculars. . . . Even little girls can be prurient teases. An eleven-year-old tells her mother that the local newsagent has exposed himself to her. It turns out she has tormented him for months, calling in for the family papers when he was alone in the shop and dancing round the back of the counter, eyes fixed on his crotch. 'I bet you my dad's is bigger than yours!' In court, the state of the penis is discussed with comic solemnity. Fully erect? Half-erect? Limp? Molested children often suffer more from this kind of questioning than from the event itself; criminal prosecution serves little purpose, though it may sharpen the atmosphere on a dull day. . . .

At five minutes past twelve the jury retire to discuss whether they wish to hear Abel Binder's defence before they deliver their verdict. To fill in time, a case is called that was heard two weeks ago and has been adjourned for sentencing. A middle-aged man who lowered his trousers under a railway bridge and attracted the attention of two girls on their way home from school.

He is a short, bald man with remarkably large, rubbery ears. These ears blush crimson as his probation officer comes forward with his social and psychiatric reports. He has a long record of similar offences, going back several years now; otherwise he seems to have led a blameless and dutiful life. He has held the same clerical job ever since leaving school; has an adequate income, a wife and three children. James, Sandra, Marilyn. The middle child is retarded. Sandra is nine but has a mental age of three years. It is since her father realised the extent of her handicap that he has begun to commit these offences. There seems no obvious connection; none is suggested. His home, five rented rooms in a converted Victorian house, is comfortable and clean. His wife has recently had an operation for varicose veins and wants the court to know that this is the only reason why she is not here today. She is fond of her husband and 'prepared to stand by him'.

All there on paper. Birth, social status, income, occupation, the amount of hire-purchase debt, the state of the furniture: his carpets and curtains are, like his history, somewhat threadbare. Imagination could supply the warp and the woof, but we are not required to exercise our imagination. Only to determine his punishment: fine, prison sentence, conditional discharge. Our sexual laws are peculiar, couched in quaint, archaic language, and presenting an awesome tariff of maximum penalties that bear little relation to the damage his offence may have done. A few inches of flesh on display that are normally hidden – but to whose harm? We are protecting our wives and daughters, our innocent children. 'Turn the telly on, little Tommy, see the daily dose of mass slaughter, smashed bones and blood, starving millions in Asia, but don't look at that dreadful man over there – he's showing his winkie!'

'Such a dreadful experience for a young girl; it could warp her for life.' Auntie's lowered voice crooned zestfully on as she bore the glad tidings to her cronies at the bridge-table. Listening outside the door, it made me laugh then – as the memory makes me laugh now: I have always been blessed with a good sense of humour and was able, even at that time, to see the funny side of the whole episode. Though, of course, if the police had actually arrested someone and confronted me with him it would have been a good deal less comic. As Steve pointed out when I told him one summer afternoon several years later. 'What would you have *done*, Pen? I mean, suppose they'd picked up some poor bloke who fitted your description exactly?'

'I'd have been in a bit of a fix, wouldn't I? Been forced to identify him?'

I said this to tease him, but he took me seriously. He was a highly serious, deeply moral young man who had taken a law degree, finished his National Service, and was about to be articled to a solicitor. My father said the legal profession would suit him, but it seemed to me (I was nearly nineteen and thought myself a good judge of character) that he was a little too easily shocked by human depravity. He said, his voice rising with horror, 'You can't mean that, Pen! That you'd have allowed them to accuse an innocent man!'

'I don't know. I honestly *don't know* what I'd have done. I think I just hoped nothing would come of it and was glad when nothing did.' I saw that this attitude, which seemed to me honest, was too light-hearted for Steve. He assumed that when people made jokes about something that troubled them they were really unfeeling. I said, 'Of course that's an understatement. I was terrified most of the time. I lived from day to day, *praying*. For a while, anyway. Oh, don't look so po-faced. I don't know why I told you!'

He sighed. 'I suppose it's the sort of thing one needs to get off one's chest.'

'I think I just wanted to make you laugh.'

'It's not funny. It can't have been at the time.'

'No. It wasn't. But sometimes you have to make yourself see the funny side. To make things more bearable.'

'Poor little Pen!' He was all sympathy now; pale gold eyes gleaming softly; full, sweet mouth smiling. 'Why do you always put up these defences? You don't have to, with me. You know, I feel really awful. If I'd known what you were going through with those ghastly people I'd have come to see you. I might even have found somewhere else for you to live! I feel dreadful now, looking back.'

'You didn't come to see me because you were angry with me about Eve. You thought what had happened was partly my fault. That was so unfair, wasn't it? If you're in a mood to feel dreadful, you should feel dreadful about that!'

'I do. I'm so sorry.'

'I hated you for ages and ages.'

'Oh, Pen. Please forgive me!'

His expression was solemnly agonised. I longed to laugh but didn't dare: I wanted his good opinion too badly. I got out of the deck-chair I was sitting in, under the apple-tree at the end of the garden, and hurled myself at him. He was propped on one elbow; I rolled him over and pinned him down on the grass he had just finished cutting. He smelled warm and pleasantly sweaty. I said, 'Silly old Steve. Your poor mamma trying to kill herself, and your foul little stepsister doing nothing to stop her! I'm not surprised you were angry. I couldn't help feeling hurt, but you couldn't help hurting me!'

What had hurt me much more was that everyone had kept the truth from me. All that long year, until my father was out of the Army and Eve out of hospital. Uncle and Auntie never mentioned Eve's illness except to say she was too sick to see anyone. Not too sick to see April, though! When I learned, later on, that she and Steve had been taken to visit their mother, I had felt so discarded, rejected. . . . Eve, whom I loved, whose love I ached for so desperately, had not wanted to see me. Only her own children; her own son, her own daughter.

I couldn't admit to Steve how unhappy this betrayal still made me. It would have shamed me too much. I said, 'If only you'd written. Just once.' I tickled his ribs, and he squawked and wriggled.

'I'm sorry,' he gasped. I stopped tickling, and he lay smiling up at me, breathing fast. 'I never meant to hurt you. Honestly. You're the last person in the world I'd want to hurt.'

His beaky face flushed suddenly. He pushed me away and sat up, combing the cut grass out of his hair with his fingers. His hand shook a little, and I noticed, with embarrassed delight, the bulge in his trousers. He drew up his knees and glanced at the house. Suppose our parents – his mother, my father – were watching this carnal romp from the window!

I said, 'What about April?'

'What about her? Oh, I see.' He grinned at me, golden eyes shining. 'I don't want to hurt her, either. Not that I imagine I *could*. But this isn't a competition!'

'You said it. You said I was *the last person.* You must have meant something.'

I pouted childishly, and he laughed, his erection subsiding. 'Don't be such a jealous baby. You are silly, Pen.'

I said, 'I'm not jealous.'

Why couldn't he have said that he loved me more than April? He must have known how I longed to come first with someone. And there was no one else; only Steve. Poor Eve was so frightened, so vulnerable, so inward-turning, she had no emotion to spare. My father was fond of me, but Eve was his chief concern, naturally; he had become such a devoted, preoccupied, *professional* husband there was no room in his life for another role.

It wasn't as if Steve owed April any brotherly loyalty. She was rarely at home; a cold, careless girl who went her own way and did what she wanted. No malice in her self-regard; it seemed a natural, impersonal force in her, like the wind or the tide. She had taken a secretarial course when she left boarding-school and was working and living in London because it was 'such a bore' trailing in from the suburbs. 'You like being at home,' she said once, when I suggested her mother might be glad of her company. 'You pushed me out years ago; you stay and get on with it.'

'I didn't push you out, April.'

'I don't hold it against you. It was a bit of luck for me, really. I can't stand sick people. I can't stand Mamma when she's down; she gets on my tits. I know why my loutish Papa bashed her up! The only way he could get some sort of response! Oh, I dare say if I thought I could do something *for* her I might feel a bit differently. But I can't, and that's all there is to it.'

I said, 'I'm not sure I can do anything, either.'

I believed I could, though. Even if Eve had no feeling for me, I loved her and believed that love and patience would heal her. Sitting holding her small, icy hands, I willed life and hope into her; a mystical power flowing across the bridge of our fingers. 'If you'd just *talk* to me, Eve. I'm sure it would help you to talk. Just tell me how you feel. Please. I'm a good listener; you don't have to worry about boring me, or anything foolish like that. Say whatever comes into your head! Even if you think it sounds cranky. And don't be ashamed, above all! Mental illness is nothing to be ashamed *of*, nowadays. We're all just sorry you feel so miserable; we don't blame you, or anything. We just simply love you and want to help you.'

But my efforts were useless. Eve's recurrent illness was a corrosive disgrace to her, a creeping rust eating away her self-confidence. She was ashamed to speak to the neighbours who knew she had been in the hospital; dreaded the days when the taxi called to take her to her outpatient appointments and she had to walk down the front path, certain that the next-door curtains were twitching. She was happier when we moved from our north London suburb to Surrey, to a cottage on the green near the asylum. I was afraid that the great Gothic tower, visible from the sitting-room window, might be a cruel and constant reminder, but she seemed to find its closeness a comfort. She was able to walk to the hospital for her therapy sessions through the leafy anonymity of Cedar Grove, carrying a basket as if she were just going shopping.

The last time this middle-aged man appeared in court for lewdly exposing his person, he was sentenced to six months' imprisonment, suspended on condition that he attended a psychiatric clinic. Unfortunately, he has not kept his appointments.

I say, 'He'd have had to take time off from his job and say why. I imagine he'd find that humiliating. People are odd about mental illness. I dare say he was afraid the other men in the office would think he was mad.'

We sit in the Judge's room considering this case. There are three of us on the Bench today: myself, the Judge, and a male magistrate with a pale, puckered face and large pale, protuberant eyes. The walls of the room are lined with leather-bound books. The law of the land, our defence against chaos. An attempt to impose order, anyway. I think: Is that why I am here? Because disorder frightens me?

'Better to be thought mad than a criminal,' the Judge says. He is quite young, firmly plump-bellied under his theatrical robe, dark-haired beneath his crimped wig.

'Sane people think so.'

'He's not insane, is he?' The Judge smiles at me patiently.

The male magistrate (whose name I did not catch earlier and do not like to ask now) sits on the edge of his chair. 'He knows what he's done, all right. You always notice one thing in these cases. They never look at you, these men! Eyes down all the time.' His own goggle eyes gleam as he gives us the benefit of this not very acute observation. 'What do they get out of it, that's what I ask myself! This chap has had plenty of chances. With respect, I'd say it was time he was taught a lesson.'

Sexual offenders have a bad time in prison; are beaten up by

37

other prisoners, kicked in the groin, fingers broken. It is the one offence criminals find unforgivable. Especially if there have been children involved. A sentimental respect for sexual innocence? Or perhaps the idea of this crime excites them. It is certainly exciting this man.

I say, 'It's not an assault case. He's never touched anyone. Girls often pretend to be more upset than they are. It's expected of them.'

'That's irrelevant, isn't it? And one can't assume it. He deliberately stationed himself near that school, didn't he? Girls have to be protected against that sort of thing. You have to think of them, don't you?'

It is clear from his eager look that he does think of them: of those round-thighed young virgins on bicycles. I wonder how his sex life would stand up to scrutiny; typed out, duplicated and passed round his judges.

I think: How would *mine?*

Eddie, stark naked, lipstick streaks decorating his high, balding forehead and pale, freckled belly, bursting out of the bathroom waving the small axe we more normally use to chop kindling, and shouting, 'I'm a wild and wicked Red Indian.'

What would that look like on paper? *This couple have been married twenty-two years, have two children. The husband enjoys boisterous sexual foreplay. It is the only way this shy, gentle man can overcome his inhibitions. But he is a conscientious, responsible parent, and since the children were born (Louise is nineteen now, Jennifer eighteen) this jolly romping has been curtailed; intercourse effectively limited to the times the children are out of the house and no one else (aunts, stepmothers, and other elderly relatives of which this family has an unusual abundance) is within earshot. Apart from some initial surprise, the wife has always accepted, and acquiesced in, these elaborate and noisy games. Telling herself humorously (she has a sense of humour, this lady, and it has sustained her through many vicissitudes) that it is all right as long as he doesn't do it in the street and frighten the horses. In her view, there is no moral objection to his behaviour. She is fond of her husband and would be prepared to stand by him should he ever appear in court for some reason, whether aberrant sexual antics or driving with excess alcohol in his bloodstream. In fact, she would defend him to the death if he were ever really in trouble, but since he is not at the moment, nor seems likely to be in the foreseeable future, she has decided to leave him. Her lover needs her more than her husband, and other people's need has always been this good woman's first thought. She feels some guilt, of course, leaving Eddie (though she pretends, out of pride, that she doesn't), but guilt has dogged her footsteps a long time, familiar as her own shadow, and she knows now she will never be rid of it. All she can do is recognise it as a useless emotion in most circumstances and harmful in some.*

Steve again. There was no blood tie, nothing incestuous in our relationship. It was his feeling that there was that did harm. Perhaps he simply felt bad because he had taken my virginity but was ashamed to admit to such an old-fashioned attitude. That I had lied to him, inventing an earlier lover (one who had 'forced' me was what I implied), was beside the point in Steve's view. Absolutely. I was younger than he was, so it must be his fault. There was something morally greedy in that, as I told him. Pinching all the responsibility, denying me any. . . .

He mopped up the blood, dried my thighs, put the towel and the sheet to soak in the basin, put fresh sheets on the bed, then lay on it, groaning. I was half-laughing, half-angry. I thumped him in the stomach and said, 'Silly Steve, *listen*. I wanted *you*. A dirty trick, a dirty, low-down, female trick. I got you worked up with that rape talk. Please, darling, forgive me.'

He said, in a hollow voice, 'I can't forgive myself, that's the trouble.'

There was no point in laughing. I said, 'Pig. Selfish pig,' turning my mouth down at the corners. Acting hurt. A hurt child.

He sat up at once, wrapping his arms round me, kissing my ear, my damp neck. 'Yes. I'm sorry. I should be thinking of you, shouldn't I? You're right, I *am* selfish. Was it all right for you? Your first time. You're so lovely.'

'I'm not. Am I?'

'See for yourself.'

He jumped off the bed and pulled me up with him, twisting me round to stand facing the long wardrobe mirror. I closed my eyes, scowling; was afraid to look at my scowling face, my plump, stocky limbs. I was so sure I was ugly; had even believed, for a time, that this was why Eve preferred her own children to me. Steve and April were tall and fair while I was short, and dark as a gipsy.

I said, in a choking voice, 'I'm too fat.'

'Rubbish.' Steve stroked my sides gently. 'Look,' he said. 'Look, my beauty.' I opened my eyes and he cupped his hand over my chin and turned my head slightly. 'Look at your face from this angle. You've got marvellous cheekbones. Like a violin.' I smiled at my reflection with bright, fixed despair, blushing and covering my full breasts with my hands. Steve let me go, laughing, and I turned, clutching him, and hid my shamed face in his warm, naked shoulder. 'Darling Steve, thank you.'

I was so grateful to him for loving me; for allowing me to love him. This was my third term at college, the end of his first year in the solicitor's office. I was reading social studies at London University and living at home with my father and Eve; he was lodging with his own father's widowed sister, his Aunt Madge in Muswell Hill. She had no children and adored Steve, who returned her affection. When his parents separated he had been hurt and unhappy, and Aunt Madge's small, cold house, crammed with unsuitably large walnut furniture, and soft, braided, bright cushions, had been an emotionally uncomplicated refuge for his sore, divided heart. He was still content there, and Aunt Madge's settled habits and innocent mind made life very easy for us. She went out two nights a week, once to the local cinema whatever was showing, once to make a fourth at mah-jong with old friends round the corner, and was delighted that I could come on those evenings to keep Steve company and 'see he ate a good supper'. Young men could not, in her view, be trusted to feed themselves without female assistance. 'Of course,' she said, wheezing with arch, asthmatic laughter, 'it would be different if you were his girl-friend, Penelope: it wouldn't be right to leave the pair of you alone then!'

I thought this old-fashioned attitude touching and funny. Aunt Madge was so sweet and absurd. And I was so happy. I felt tied to Steve for the rest of our lives. What could possibly part us? We would get married, have two boys and two girls (I dreamed about these children while I took notes during lectures, named and renamed them), grow old together. Those bi-weekly evenings I left college early, caught a slow, swaying bus and sat smiling at my reflection in the dark window; a plump, eager, plain girl grown beautiful with love.

I worshipped Steve. Nothing he did could be wrong, since everything about him was perfect. He was cleverer than I was, more honest, much kinder. Even his slowness to laughter was a proper rebuke to my facile frivolity. I tried to be what he seemed to want me to be: grave and good. Tried to see, when he frowned at my silly joke about Aunt Madge's asthma ('If she should come back unexpectedly, we'd have time to get dressed. That chest of hers is like the alarm-clock in the crocodile's tummy in *Peter Pan*, isn't it?'), that it really was rather tasteless to make fun of her disability. Even when it became clear that Aunt Madge's opinion was of crucial importance to him, I could not see this as weakness on his part, even though he confessed it.

'I know it's dreadful trivial of me, but I feel so uncomfortable, darling. I wake up at night, sweating. Not just at her coming in and catching us at it – that would be farcical – but at what she would *think* if she knew!'

I said, uncomprehending, 'Why don't we tell her we love each other and mean to get married?'

He looked so amazed I couldn't help laughing. I said, 'Oh, I know we can't *yet*! I only meant let her know we are going to, when we can afford it. Though of course we could manage now, if I left college. We don't have to wait till you're qualified. Even without a degree, I could earn something, couldn't I?' My capacity for sacrifice, unused but unlimited, excited me. I would scrub floors for Steve! Anything! If only he'd let me. He was so conventional in some ways. Husbands supporting wives and wives in the kitchen and all that out-of-date nonsense. But I could persuade him. I faced him exultantly. 'I really don't mind what I do, Steve. I'll be an office cleaner. Or a lavatory attendant. Just as long as we can be together.'

He said, 'But we can't be!' He sighed through clenched teeth, tugged at his rumpled, fair hair. 'Pen. Darling Pen, that's my *point*. Aunt Madge would be shattered! Brother and sister – Oh, I know we aren't really, but that's how she'd look at it. And not just Aunt Madge. Everyone. Your father, my mother. Don't you see?'

I heard what he said, but what I saw – understood – was quite different. He didn't love me. How stupid I'd been to think otherwise. And how brave of him to admit it. How honest! Well, I could be brave, too! I stood, back to the door in his small, crowded bedroom – lowering wardrobe, vast, walnut-frame bed, huge oil-painting of a storm-tossed tea-clipper on a dark sea – and took it on the chin, head up, spine straight, like a soldier.

'I don't blame you for not loving me. Heaven above!' I gave a loud, cracked, unnatural laugh. 'I wouldn't love me if I were you.'

This wasn't meant to be bitter. I didn't feel bitter, just foolish. What folly, to imagine this gentle, fastidious man was in love with me! I wasn't worth loving; so stupid, so clumsy! In a strange way, his rejection of me made me value him more. It proved he was too good for me. That he was as far above me as the stars.

'Darling Pen.' He held out his hands, palm upwards, then let them fall helplessly. His expression was helpless, his face drained of colour under the hideous, unshaded, overhead light. He said, 'But of course I love you. It's just that it's so bloody impossible. Unfair to you to go on. When I get married, *if* I get married, I want things to be perfect – and they never could be for us.'

Not only brave, but also kind. Trying to let me down lightly. His sweet magnanimity moved me almost to tears. I said hoarsely, 'It's all right. I'm not going to cry or make a scene. Really. So don't worry. *Please*. I'll get over it. The worst thing would be to feel you were worrying. I want you to be happy – that's *all* I want, Steve. Except – well, we can see each other sometimes, can't we? Not just when you come home. On our own, now and then? I won't bother you. I mean, I won't expect you to *kiss* me, or anything. Though if you wanted to – well, you could. Whatever you feel like. If you can't bear to see me, then that's all right, too.'

'Oh God!' Steve closed his eyes briefly. To shut out the sight of me? The reproach of my shining, masochist's face? He said, with resentment and pity, 'I'm sorry, Pen. I didn't mean it to end like this. I'd no idea you thought we could really get married. I am an unimaginative, selfish shit. And a coward too, which is worse in the circumstances. Since I love you, I mean. But I can't change myself. I know I shouldn't care so much what people think, but I *do*.'

'One has to consider public opinion in this sort of case,' the Judge says, speaking not about Steve, but about the bald, large-eared man with a wife and three children, one of them mentally backward, waiting in their five clean rented rooms for the husband and father who will not return to them for a while. It would be perverse not to bring the suspended sentence into operation. It was imposed by a previous court for a similar offence and his circumstances have not changed in any legally relevant way.

I say, 'When people talk about public opinion, they don't mean what *they* think, necessarily, or what their friends think, but the opinions of some old, respectable aunt.'

'Do you think old, respectable aunts should not be listened to?' The Judge smiles politely. He knows about compassionate lady magistrates, that smile says; all their soft-hearted arguments.

I am stung. Does he think *I* am not worth listening to? I say sharply, 'People are always talking about public opinion as if it were something quite simple you could go and look up in a library. But it's often just a term to shelter behind. To avoid examining an irrational attitude. And our attitude towards sex offenders is pretty irrational, isn't it? We're sending this poor man to prison; but if he were a dangerous driver, and much more of a real threat, likely to *kill* someone after all, he'd be getting off with a fine.'

The Judge nods. He looks at me thoughtfully; so long and steadily that I begin to wish I had kept my mouth shut. What a pompous ass I am, laying down the law to this professional! I expect a chilly reply, a put-down, but instead he smiles suddenly – a real smile this time – and says, 'People are more frightened of sex than of death, perhaps. Do you think that's the answer?'

Of course I had frightened Steve. Scared him rigid. My lusty, gusty emotion blowing him helplessly along like a leaf in a storm when he needed stillness and calm, time to recover, for raw wounds to heal. He had had so much to hide for so long. A mother not only mad but (almost worse for a self-conscious, sensitive boy) called by a different name from his own when she married my father. Shame and fear had haunted Steve through his schooldays, leaving him with a morbid dread of being caught out, of what people thought of him, how they judged what he did. However innocent his behaviour, he would always feel guilty. . . .

I think: *April!* Had she really said, 'You pushed me out years ago'? Or is that my own sense of guilt speaking? Hindsight unfairly distorting memory. It wasn't altogether for my sake that

44

April had been sent to boarding-school, surely? She had always been difficult; a loud, turbulent child, full of great, windy rages. Contemptuous of Eve, who 'couldn't control her'. So Aunt Madge said. Adding, 'I'm afraid April takes after her father.'

Steve and April's father, Aunt Madge's brother; a hard, boozy, promiscuous man who had passed his wilfulness and sexual appetites on to his daughter. But the kind of behaviour Aunt Madge might condone in a man she naturally condemned in a girl. 'I'm afraid she's had it coming a long time' was Aunt Madge's comment when she heard that April was pregnant. This was one evening when the local cinema was showing an old film she had seen twice before and she stayed at home to have supper with Steve and me. We had not been lovers long. We sat, picking at cold meat and salad, listening to Aunt Madge, and holding hands furtively under the table. 'She'll be lucky if he marries her, if you ask me,' Aunt Madge pronounced. 'Once a man's had what he wants in that way from a woman, he loses respect for her.'

An absurd platitude (Steve and I exchanged sly, amused glances), but it turned out sadly true. The father of April's child was a Polish airman, a fighter pilot who had flown with the Royal Air Force during the war and settled here afterwards. He had picked April up in a pub and taken her to bed the same night. Although she had always had plenty of boy-friends, and given everyone who knew her an impression of what Aunt Madge called 'wildness', this man was in fact her first lover. He married April when she was six months pregnant and despised her because she was not a virgin at the time of the ceremony. He didn't touch her until the boy, Adam, was born; a month later, he hit her for the first time.

They were living three floors up in an old terrace-house in Fulham. They had two cluttered rooms and a bath in the kitchen. There was nowhere to dry clothes except on a line over the bath; the place smelled of damp napkins and vegetable refuse. The sour air met me as I climbed the stairs, my arms full of fruit and flowers, and I wondered if April would think me a busybody if I offered to clear up a bit. I walked into the sitting-room, saw her bruised mouth and cheek, and knew she needed more help than that. She said, 'Charles bashed me up, the rotten, lousy bastard,' and I felt, first, a shocked thrill of excitement and then (though April, tearless and angry, hardly invited it) a warm, orgasmic rush of real pity. April had always been my rival, my enemy, cold and implacable; now, looking at her poor, damaged face, I saw she was vulnerable. She had grown thin since her marriage and the child's birth; although she was still coarser-featured than Steve, her hollowed eyes and prominent nose made her look more like him than she had done before. I began, from that moment, to love her. I cried indignantly, 'Poor darling, how awful! Whatever made him do that?'

'The man in the bottom flat helped me haul the bloody pram up the front steps and carried my shopping upstairs. I asked him in for a coffee. Charles met him on the way out.'

'And hit you? Oh, April!'

'Well, you know what he thought. I told him we were drinking coffee, not fucking, but he still hit me. I couldn't stop him; I was holding the baby.'

'Oh, poor little Adam!'

'He started to yell, luckily. Otherwise bloody Charles would have broken my jaw.' She grinned at me coldly. 'Don't look so shocked! Some of the women round here would think that was normal!'

'But it's dreadful. . . .'

'Charles doesn't think so. It's the right way to treat whores, he'd say. I've been a whore to him from the beginning. Now I'm a whore *and* a cow. A milk-cow for his baby. That's why he married me. He wanted a son. Now he's got one, he doesn't want me.'

'That can't be true, April.'

'You mean, it's not *pleasant*?'

'No. But you're upset. Anyone would be! It's frightful of him to hit you, of course, but it doesn't mean he doesn't love you. Just

the opposite, really. If he was jealous. Or had he been drinking? I expect he was sorry. . . .'

I thought of Steve suddenly; an erotic fantasy in which he was beating me, then crawling and kissing my feet in apology. Confused, I bent over the cot and crooned at the baby. He was awake, sucking his fist with a moist, smacking sound.

April said, 'Little Miss Sunshine.'

She smiled at me sadly. Her remarkable eyes – tawny in some lights, pale gold in others – looked bloodshot and dull. 'There were stains down the front of her dress. She said, 'It's nice of you to visit me in this ghastly slum. Would you like something? A cup of tea? Or a gin? Charles hardly ever drinks, as it happens – or not at home anyway – but I do sometimes.' She looked vaguely about her as if she half-expected a bottle of gin to materialise out of the air.

I said, 'It's all right. I don't want anything.' The baby had stopped sucking his fist and was whimpering. I said, 'Can I pick him up, April?'

'You can feed him, if you like. I don't have much milk at the six o'clock feed so I sometimes give him an illicit bottle.'

'Illicit?' The adjective seemed a strange one to use.

'Well,' April said. 'Charles. . . .'

She stopped, audibly catching her breath. Running steps were heard on the stairs; the door opened. Charles entered, closed it behind him. A short neatly made man with a full, pink-and-white face and bright eyes like dark, polished stones. He said, 'So we have a visitor!' He crossed the room, took my hand and lifted it to his mouth, lightly brushing it with his lips. I felt his warm breath on my fingers. He smiled at me. The skin of his face was smooth and unmarked like the skin of a young healthy girl. Or a wax model. He said, 'I didn't know you were coming.'

The baby began to whimper again, more demandingly. Charles said, without looking at April, 'It is time for his feed.'

April had not moved since he came in; had barely seemed to

47

be breathing. Now she sat in a low chair by the cot and picked the child up. She fumbled clumsily with the buttons that fastened her dress, slipped a strap off her shoulders, thrust her brown nipple into the baby's mouth. Her long hair fell forward and hid her face, but her fingers, compressing the soft flesh of her breast, were visibly trembling. The baby sucked for a minute, then twisted his head away and wailed thinly.

Charles said, quietly and angrily, 'You haven't been drinking.'

I misunderstood this accusation. Gin, presumably, was bad for babies. Alcohol in the mother's bloodstream passed into the milk. Could babies get drunk? I said, 'No. Really she hasn't, Charles. I mean, she offered me a drink but we didn't have one.'

He ignored me. I might not have spoken. April pressed her nipple into the baby's mouth, and again he rejected it. His cry became desperate. April lifted her head and looked at Charles dumbly. She was sweating. I could smell her sweat; the air seemed full of it suddenly. The rank scent of fear.

Charles turned on his heels and marched from the room. He left the door open. We heard a tap running. He came back, carrying a large blue-and-white jug and a full glass of water still cloudy with the force of the jet from the tap. He said, 'You do not drink enough. I have told you so many times. Drink now, and the milk will come in.'

April drank. Her long white throat shuddered convulsively as if it hurt her to swallow. When she had emptied the glass, Charles refilled it from the blue-and-white jug. She drank half the water and stopped. 'Finish it,' Charles commanded. She drank again; small sips with deep, effortful breaths in between. Charles said, 'Do you feel the milk coming in yet?' and, when she shook her head, filled the glass again. April whispered, 'I can't manage any more. Not for a minute or two. I'll be sick. . . .'

Charles said, 'The boy is hungry now. Must he wait for your pleasure?'

There were tears in April's eyes as she lifted the glass to her

lips. They seemed an inadequate response to the menace that suddenly seemed to be filling the room with an almost tangible
presence; a leaden weight that pressed hard on my chest. I fought
against it, made myself breathe, felt the air expanding my lungs.
My mouth was dry. I said, 'Don't be ridiculous, Charles,' and
speaking these words gave me courage. The situation *was*
ridiculous – no more than that! They were both overwrought and
exhausted. No doubt there had been sleepless nights with the baby
waking and crying. Of course Charles should not have hit April,
but he was a jealous man, a hot-blooded foreigner, and April had
probably provoked him. She could look and sound so brazen
sometimes! This silly scene was simply an extension of a degrading
but equally silly quarrel. They must make it up. I must help them.
I said, 'She can't feed Adam if she's bullied, can she? And you
are being a bit of a bully, Charles, really!' I laughed, to lighten
this reprimand, and felt I had struck the right note. 'Suppose I go
and make us all a nice cup of tea? We could give Adam a bottle to
keep him quiet for a while, and April could feed him later.'

Charles said, 'I do not want tea. And my son will not have a
bottle, now or at any other time. His mother will feed him.'

He took the child from April's lap and carried him to a
weighing machine that stood on a table against the wall. The baby
screamed and kicked thin, purple legs loose from his wrappings
as his father adjusted the weights until the balance was perfect.
April watched tensely, hunched forward in her low nursing-chair,
one veined breast dangling, I saw a drop of bluish liquid ooze
from the nipple, and a wave of hot relief washed over me and
receded, leaving me cold and trembling. April took a clean napkin
that hung over the sides of the cot and held it against her. She had
closed her eyes and was swaying slightly – a condemned criminal,
I thought, reprieved at the very last moment! Charles put the baby
back on her lap, and she bowed her head humbly over him as he
started to suck, one tiny hand spread like a pink starfish on her
pale breast. Her husband stood to attention beside her, looking

down at her bent head and frowning. For several minutes there was no sound in the room except the baby's soft, rhythmic sucking. Then Charles said, 'When you have fed him, I will weigh him again and see how much he has taken. He should have five ounces at least at this feed. You have not been resting as I told you to do; that is the trouble. Visitors are not good for you. You should rest in the afternoons, not giggle and gossip; and take plenty to drink, then you will be able to feed him.' He looked at me with his dark, stony eyes. 'I am sorry to be inhospitable, but it is best for a mother to be alone at these times.'

I stood up. My muscles were aching as if after some violent physical effort. I felt weak and foolish and frightened and angry. I had been wrong about this being a silly scene. What I had witnessed was absurd, of course, but it was horrible too – a horrible piece of deliberate, cold cruelty. I didn't know what to do – whether to go or to stay. What would Charles do if April couldn't supply her child with five ounces of milk? Presumably he wouldn't hit her while I was there. On the other hand, if my presence annoyed him, he might set about both of us. His behaviour hardly seemed rational. I said carefully, 'I'll come again, April, shall I?' and when she looked up with a small nod, a shamed smile, I was astonished to find how grateful I felt for this clear dismissal. It was dreadful to see April humiliated, and I was afraid for her as well as sorry, but my strongest emotion at that particular moment was fear for myself. Charles opened the door for me and I felt my flesh shrink as I scuttled past him. I was physically terrified, as I would have been of an uncertain and dangerous animal. . . .

In domestic courts evidence of cruelty is hard to get for precisely this reason. A violent husband is only too likely to beat up a compassionate neighbour. Even the victim will sometimes turn on her rescuer. A man knocks his wife about on the street; a young Galahad gallops up and fells the coarse brute with a blow. To his amazement, the woman screams abuse at him for attacking her loved one, bashes him round the head with her heavy handbag, tries to scratch his eyes out. Her impetuous defender retires sadder and wiser, nursing his injuries. No wonder that much of the time people pass by on the other side, close their windows and turn up the radio, tell each other that the mayhem next door is none of their business. Even if they call the police, once in court the case often crumbles. Bruises have faded, burning indignation has cooled and the process of law is too slow and deliberate to breathe fire into ashes. There are absurd arguments about the weapon used, the thickness of the stick, the belt or the rope. Humiliated wives change their evidence, lie for any one of a hundred reasons. The reactions of the Bench can be complex, too. The offending husband, cleaned up for the occasion and dressed in his best suit, rarely looks like a lout. No sympathy with his alleged behaviour, of course, but it can be true sometimes that the bad man does what the good man dreams. To some of his judges, the defendant may look uncomfortably like a scapegoat: he has acted out the violence they have only imagined when their wives have nagged them, deceived them with other men, backed the new car into a lamp standard, or simply grown old or unwanted or ugly. And, apart from these private referrals, a domestic dispute is always a difficult matter. You need to be wise as Solomon to adjudicate fairly. A sense of resentment at being landed with an impossible task is sometimes worked off on those few hardy witnesses who have been persuaded to come to the court. What sort of person comes between husband and wife in this way? Busybodies, do-gooders – the general feeling is that their motives are to some extent doubtful. If the witness is a woman, perhaps her own marriage is on the rocks and she has been making mischief to ease her own pain. Unhappy people like to see others unhappy. Who knows – this unfortunate couple might have worked things out between them if she had not interfered, stirred the pot. And sometimes even cruder accusations are made. A neighbour gives evidence. She has seen marks on the poor woman next door, heard her cries. The man is a handsome brute with a bold, roving eye. His lawyer suggests that the witness is jealous. She fancies this fellow herself, perhaps? A clever advocate will not actually say this, of course, simply imply it with a faint smile, a quizzical lift of the eyebrow.

I didn't 'fancy' Charles. Or not at that time. If there was an element of sexual excitement in my horrified pity for April, I was unaware of it. And, although I was hurt and bewildered because Steve had just ended our love affair, I felt no pleasure in seeing proud April brought low. It seemed almost wicked to think of my own situation when hers was so much more terrible. A romantic indulgence to feel that defending April was one way to stay close to Steve, one way to serve him. When I caught my thoughts straying that way – dreaming that April might tell him sometime what a wonderful comfort I was to her – I marshalled them sternly like a sergeant-major controlling sloppy recruits on parade. *Get back in line there! Eyes front! Pick up your rifle!* I marched into battle on April's behalf, banners flying, trumpets sounding. A soldier with a righteous cause, defending the weak, strengthening the faint-hearted.

April was so *defeated*! I could hardly credit the change in her. It was as if fear and physical weakness had worked on her like a bad fairy's spell, changing her from a strong, confident, healthy girl into a creature so helpless and hopeless that she could not be expected to fend for herself. Once she knew I was ready to act as her champion, she seemed quite content to let me sit back and do all the fighting. I told myself this was just self-preservation. Safety, for oppressed people, often lies in passivity – although they may hope for deliverance, they will continue to appease their oppressors until it is certain – but April's attitude towards Charles seemed more ambivalent than that. A strange, sacrificial madness. She said, 'You might as well face it. Poles are different from us. All that crappy stuff about family honour really means something to them. Women are one thing – a free fuck's always welcome – but wives should come pure to their marriage-bed, or how can you trust them?' Or 'He may be a ghastly husband by your standards, Pen, but he's a bloody marvellous lover.' Or 'He really does care for the baby.'

None of these arguments was an adequate excuse for staying with a man who behaved so atrociously. Nor did they sound to me like excuses. If April had really wanted to stay with her husband, she would surely have made some attempt to conceal the signs of his violence which increased as the months passed. Instead, she flaunted them like honourable scars, wore low-necked dresses to show off the marks on her throat, never tried to hide a puffy eye or a swollen lip with dark glasses or make-up. Quite in character with the old April who scorned pretences, perhaps, but it seemed to me like a cry for help. She wanted to leave Charles, of course she did – as long as someone else would take the responsibility! She was incapable, now, of making a move on her own. Fear had drained out her spirit; she was frightened of freedom. She said, 'Where would we go, for Christ's sake? There's the *baby*! What the hell would we live on?'

'I'd help you, April. We'd manage somehow. We could find a flat. I could leave college, get a job of some sort. Or you could, and I could look after Adam. There's a girl on my course who brings her baby to lectures. She carries him on her back in a sort of canvas sling. He's no trouble.'

We were sitting, this golden summer afternoon, in a small, dusty park near April's flat. I bent over the pram and tickled Adam's stomach. He kicked his brown, dimpled legs and laughed up at me, long-lashed eyes gleaming darkly. The thought of looking after him as if he were my own baby was a prospect so sweet it made my heart flutter. I said, 'He'd be all right with me. He loves me already – don't you, my angel? And you've got to think of *him*, April! You can't go on like this, for his sake! It's an appalling situation for a child to grow up in. He needs love and security, not rows and blows.' The truth of this struck me suddenly with terrifying force. I saw, as in a vivid film-flash, the little boy wailing and clutching the bars of his cot while his parents roared round him; two brawling giants, fists and oaths flying.

April said, 'I could do with a bit of that myself. Love and security.' She laughed angrily, and I thought she hadn't altered so much if she could still put her own needs and feelings before anyone else's. Even before her own child's! Poor little Adam, I thought, poor, doomed baby – and then realised with a gloriously invigorating access of energy that at least he had me to save him! I would save him, and April too. They were both dependent on me, and I would not let them down. I looked at April's tired face and told myself that, although her cold self-regard was shocking, it was quite understandable and even, in a sense, reassuring: it meant she had not been totally crushed. Of course Charles had done her great emotional damage, but she was resilient by nature. Once she had broken loose, she would begin to recover. . . .

She said abruptly, 'It's no good, you know.'

'What's no good, dear?'

'This idea of yours about setting up house together. Two bloody women! Even if we could manage the money side, we'd be at each other's throats in no time.'

'Why on earth should we? We're fond of each other.' This seemed presumptuous. I added quickly, 'I'm fond of *you*, anyway. And there's no reason except silly convention why two girls shouldn't be able to bring up a baby.'

April wriggled her shoulders and sighed. 'Oh, for God's sake, Pen. It wouldn't work because I need a *man*. Not just for bed. I can't bear other women, if you must know. Not at close quarters, anyway. I had enough at that boarding-school. All those girls nattering and twittering on like a bloody nest full of sparrows. Gas-fires and gossip! Men suit me better.'

I forbore to point out that it was a man who was responsible for April's present plight, for her misery and despair, for her physical danger. 'If you mean you want another husband, you won't find one if you stay with Charles, will you?' I thought that there was a sound, practical way in which April's instincts were right. Charles might continue to threaten her if there was no man around to send him packing! I said, 'You could come home. Eve's on an even keel at the moment. And Father would be there if Charles turned up to make trouble.'

My father had retired early from the Civil Service in order to spend more time with Eve. He would be glad to have someone else in the house when he wanted to play golf, or billiards at the club with his cronies. And the baby would be good for Eve, too. It seemed to me sometimes that half her trouble was lack of occupation. My father did most of the work in the house while she sat with idle hands, staring out of the window. The more I thought about it, the more it seemed the ideal solution for everyone. 'There would always be someone to look after Adam; you could get out and about, meet people, do a part-time job if you wanted to. I know the house is small, but you could have my room – I don't mind. I can sleep in the boxroom. And it'll be good for Adam to have a garden to play in when he's a bit older. The people we bought the house from had young children and there's an old sandpit. We can get some fresh sand. And Father can fix up a swing for him under the apple-tree.'

'Oh God,' April said.

'What's wrong, dear?'

'I don't know.' She shook her head fretfully. 'The way you rush on, I suppose. Sandpits and swings! You make me feel breathless.'

I said, 'You're exhausted, poor darling. And I'm not surprised, either. But once you've made up your mind you'll feel better. It always works like that. Indecision is terribly tiring.'

'Made up my mind to what?'

'To leave Charles, of course.'

April stared at me stupidly. Her mouth hung open a little; her hair was harsh, like dry strands of wheat bleached in the sun. It had lost colour as her face had lost beauty. She looked heavy and dull and much older. I felt exultant because I was so young and strong beside her. I said, 'You know you must, don't you? Things can only get worse. He'll kill you one day. Or at least do you some frightful injury. You know that you're scared of him. I've seen you cringe as he walks in the door. It's simply not tolerable. No one could expect you to tolerate it.'

She said slowly, 'I haven't the strength to go, that's the trouble. The sheer bloody *mechanics* of it. All too much – I can't cope with anything. I just want to crawl into a corner and cover my head up and *die*.'

'Oh, my poor love!' I sat beside her, put my arm round her shoulders, drew her against me, stroked her stiff hair. She made a small, muffled sound, half a laugh, half a whimper. I said, 'Don't cry, darling. It won't be too hard, I promise you. I'll see to it all. I'll come in a taxi after Charles has left for the office. We'll pack up together. Or I'll do it – you needn't do anything. Just sit quiet and tell me what you want to take with you. We can leave Charles a note if you like, but we don't have to let him know where you are. It might be best not to. We'll see a solicitor and let him deal with that side of things. He'll tell you what's best. And it shouldn't be difficult. We've got enough evidence to divorce Charles twenty times over!'

April said, 'You sound like Queen Victoria! That royal "We"!' She moved out of my arms and sat up straight, smiling. The smile lifted the lines of her face and made her look young again. The light had returned to her eyes and they shone like new pennies. She said, 'You are sweet, Pen. I am grateful, truly. But I simply can't do it. It's simply not possible. They won't want me at home. Not my mamma, nor your father!'

'But of course they will, darling,' I cried. 'It's your home, isn't it?'

My father said, 'Oh God, Pen.'

He sat beside Eve on the chintz-covered sofa in their small

drawing-room. The weather had broken late in the afternoon; steely spring hailstones lashed the window, and the sky gleamed with a livid light that made him look yellow and haggard. He had lost weight recently; his collar was loose round his neck. How retirement had aged him, I thought. A few months ago he had been a strong man in his prime. Now he was an old one, with grey hair, and mottled veins on his cheeks, eyeing me with alarm and resentment as if I had threatened him. He said, in a horrified voice, 'Surely things aren't as bad as that! I should have thought April was able to look after herself in most situations.' He gave a cracked chuckle. 'An Iron Maiden. I'd have put my money on her, I must say, in a matrimonial scrap.'

I said, 'Of course she didn't want you to know how unhappy she was. You know how proud she is. But she really is desperate. I wouldn't have suggested her coming here otherwise. I'm sorry if you think I was wrong.'

Eve said, 'Your father's not been well lately, Pen. April and Adam – well, they might be too much for him.'

She smiled at my father and held out her skinny hand. He took it and placed it tenderly on his bony knee. They sat, holding hands, and regarding me with an air of joint, nervous apology.

I was shocked by their attitude, even though I thought that I understood it. Old people were often selfish, and these two, perhaps, had more reason than most. Eve's illness had cut them off from the world; they lived for each other, protected each other. . . .

I said, 'But this is April's *home*, isn't it? Oh, I can see she and Adam might disturb your cosy routine. But where else can she go? Who else can she turn to?'

My father said, 'Being a parent doesn't entail providing life cover. One can't be responsible for one's children for ever.'

'You never have been, for April! I mean, she never had a real home after you and Eve married, did she? It makes me feel dreadfully guilty, whenever I think of it.'

'I don't think you need carry that particular burden,' my father said mildly.

'Oh, but I *do*. It was my fault she was packed off to boarding-school, wasn't it? Even if I didn't realise it at the time, I know it was my fault *now*, and I can't help feeling ashamed. It must have been dreadful for her, seeing another little girl take her place in her mother's affections; and you don't know, if that hadn't happened, if she'd had a more secure childhood, she might not be in this awful mess now! That's why I feel I must do my best to make it up to her, make amends if I can. I should have thought you'd both have felt the same way! And want to see the same kind of thing doesn't happen to Adam. Your first husband knocked you about, didn't he, Eve? Didn't that upset your children, poor Steve, and April? Don't you want to spare your grandson that kind of experience? I'm terribly afraid that, if he isn't rescued quite soon, he'll be ruined for life! You might as well chuck him on the scrap-heap like a piece of unwanted old rubbish and make an end of it.'

Replaying that scene in my mind – hearing, as on some old gramo-phone record, that deedy, didactic young voice ranting on – I shudder and squirm. What frightful emotional blackmail! How thoughtless, how basically stupid, how cruel! And yet (I am, after all, trying to be honest and fair to myself) the passionate feelings that prompted me to bully Eve and my father into submission were decent and genuine. As were the arguments I used, which are the same arguments I hear almost every time I am presented with a sympathetic social report in the courts. Men who beat up their wives, women who batter their children (breaking skulls, snap-ping bones), have been beaten up, battered by their fathers and mothers in childhood. Cruelty breeds cruelty as crime and ignor-ance and poverty breed crime and ignorance and poverty.

Not that, in a practical sense, it helps much to know this. (I am not sure I helped Adam, as it turned out, though I may have spared his wife a few bruises.) There is no obvious way to break the fixed pattern, no easy road back into Eden.

The sexual offender stands up in the dock as we return to the court. Perhaps he still hopes as he looks at our faces, but he must know he has had plenty of 'chances'. More than he should have had, in some people's view. Now we have come to the end of our patience, and he will be driven away in a closed van and locked up. His possessions will be taken away, his fingerprints filed. He will be allowed to send and receive two letters a week. If his wife can afford the fare and find someone to take care of the children, she will be able to visit him. He will be fed, attend chapel, work in the prison laundry or at some simple industrial task. It will cost, at present prices, something over two thousand pounds a year to spare society the sight of his penis, another thousand or so to support his wife and his children. He will, almost certainly, lose his job, the respect of his neighbours, his pitiful hopes for the future. He should have thought of all that before, perhaps.

I cannot look at him as the Judge pronounces his sentence. I am ashamed of my part in this shameful exercise. I am also ashamed of being ashamed: it seems intellectually sloppy. A device to let myself off, wash my hands. I watch the sun shifting across the wall of the court-room and wonder who will tell his wife that he has been taken to prison. Is she on the telephone? Probably not. The probation officer will call on her later today. Or a social worker. Whoever goes will be kind: this unfortunate woman has just had an operation for varicose veins, and little Sandra is mentally backward. Lucky for Sandra, in one way: she will not understand what has happened. How will her mother tell the other two children? What will she say to them? I think of myself, laying the table for tea in my own sunny kitchen, making peanut-butter sandwiches and listening for the *ting* of bicycle-bells, the scrape of wheels on the gravel. Louise and Jenny, home from afternoon school. Two plump little girls with square, pale, freckled faces and Eddie's small, anxious eyes, his shy habit of blinking with concerned effort before asking a question. 'Where's Daddy?' 'I'm afraid Daddy won't be home for a while. He's had to go on a business trip.' Or 'You must be brave, darlings. Your father has gone to prison.' It would depend, of course, on how old they are. If they are ten and twelve (this is the age they are in my mind at the moment, the age when they always wanted peanut butter for tea), I will probably tell them the truth. Children cannot always be protected, and if I help them to face this disaster bravely they may even benefit from it, grow strong and sturdy through suffering. Tears prickle my eyes, a lump rises up in my throat as this noble thought strikes me and I act out this sad scene, comfort my daughters. 'We must comfort each other, my darlings, but first of all we must think of poor Daddy.' They cry, and their tears give me some satisfaction. I love them, they are my dear, good, helpful children, never a moment's anxiety, but sometimes they seem a bit dull to me, a bit unresponsive, and I love them more when they weep: it shows that they need me. I embrace them tenderly. 'Don't cry, my babies. We must be sorry for Daddy, not for ourselves. Be brave for his sake and never stop loving him. He needs us to love him now more than ever before.'

I think: What bloody rubbish! This bleeding-heart fantasy (occupying, in present time, no more than a fraction of a second, like a dream before waking) is a pathetic irrelevance. Easy enough to tell children their father has gone to prison. Explaining why is the problem. The nub of the matter, the nitty-gritty. For this flasher's wife, anyway. What can she say? Daddy has been naughty – he took off his trousers in public?

The Judge has finished speaking. The man in the dock does not move, makes no sound. I think: Why doesn't he shout, scream, tear at his cheeks with his fingernails, make some protest that will force us all to realise the enormity of what we are doing to him! It is amazing (at least it amazes me) how rarely scenes of this kind take place. Perhaps the defendant has already endured, in his mind, everything that can possibly happen to him and so, when the moment comes and his fate is revealed, actually feels little beyond exhausted indifference. There is only one sign that this man has even heard the Judge's pronouncement. His ears – those elephantine absurdities, jutting out on either side of his otherwise inconspicuous, everyday face – have gone scarlet. Their deep crimson colour makes them look false; joke ears, worn by a clownish comedian trying to amuse the kiddies in a Christmas pantomime. When he was young, those ears must have meant an exquisite martyrdom. Was he called 'Dumbo' in the school playground? Laughed at by silly girls, tortured by bigger boys, great virile bullies with small ears and moustaches? Growing up desperate to show them that he was, in some respects, as normal as they were? His penis, at least, is not freakish! Some such physical weakness (a hormonal deficiency, if not those huge ears) may have brought him to this sad pass. Or perhaps his problem is an emotional one. He has fathered a handicapped child. Not his fault, he is mutely proclaiming as he exposes his fine, healthy organ; it is clear the blame lies elsewhere.

I am sorry for him, naturally. But the structural failures of his wretched life are not my concern. I am not a psychiatrist, nor a novelist, nor a social worker, nor God; my job (which I have, after all, taken on voluntarily) is to deal with effects, not with causes. If it distresses me more than usual on this occasion, it is not just because I dislike sending people to prison, feel suffocating panic at the thought of locked doors and high walls, nor is it altogether on this man's account. His particular crime is not one I could ever commit (even if I had the equipment I cannot imagine myself wanting to), but there is a more general sense in which I feel my own life is on trial today. Someone has sent me twenty aspirins in a brown envelope, and that anonymous accusation rumbles on in the depths of my mind like a monotonous and menacing drum, sharpening my sympathies with all accused persons, alerting my memory, forcing me to examine my own failures, seek out my own guilt. Or establish my innocence, rather. I am a law-abiding, law-enforcing woman who has always tried to act decently. I am leaving my husband, but there is nothing illegal in that, nothing criminal. And, as far as the moral issue goes, I can only say that I am doing what honestly seems to me the right thing at this moment. No one can say I have not done my duty by Eddie. Or can they? Perhaps this is what's troubling me. My trial is a private one – I am my own judge, my own jury – but I would really prefer to be acquitted in public. Not only innocent, but openly seen to be.

I almost envy Abel Binder, who has replaced the sexual offender in the dock. At least he will leave this court without a stain on his character! Even Goggle Eyes, who seems suspicious by nature, agrees that he never meant to steal that wrecked car. Crazy to lie to the police, of course, but he had paid for that lie a hundred times over. Terrible to be accused, when you know you are innocent. And even though his counsel will have reassured him, explained that, after the Judge's quite clear direction, the jury are bound to acquit him, this must be a tense moment for Abel. He stands in the centre of the stage, the unwilling star of this drama, and a dusty sun-shaft seeks him out like a spotlight. He puts his hands up to his eyes, and the usher crosses the floor of the court and lowers the blind.

The jury sit, waiting. The elderly man coughs into his handkerchief and looks up at the Judge with an apologetic expression. The woman in the fur-collared coat is feeling the heat; she is breathing in little puffs; her unpowdered face glistens. A younger woman touches her hair and smiles secretly. She is pretty and sexy with sharp little nipples poking out the thin stuff of her blouse. The eyes of the man next to her roll shyly towards them.

The foreman stands up. He is very short, very broad, with long arms that sweep forward from roundly hunched shoulders, and dark, narrow-set eyes in the face of an honest ape. His yellow silk shirt and expensive jacket explain why he has been chosen to act as spokesman rather than the obvious labourer behind him in his cheap, decent suit. And they would, of course, choose a *man*! I think this with some indignation as I look at what seems to me the

Part Two

more obvious choice: a middle-aged woman with an alert, composed, intelligent face. A senior civil servant, or perhaps a headmistress – she has the air of someone who is used to making decisions and seeing them carried out. Watching her, admiring her neat, tan-coloured wool dress, I see she is frowning and, in the same instant, know why; realise, even before the foreman begins to speak in his educated slightly nasal, upper-class voice, that the jury have either misunderstood or rejected the Judge's direction. They do not intend to acquit or convict Abel Binder until they have heard his defence.

'Bloody juries,' I say.

'If you ever found yourself in a fix, you might be glad to be tried by one.' The Judge buys me a sherry from the bar and tells me a story. Two judges in a train, watching a fox in a field, hard on the heels of a zig-zagging rabbit. One judge says to the other, 'That's the end of that rabbit, except for the grace of God, or a British jury.'

This is not the first time I have heard this apocryphal tale. I look down my nose and smile dutifully.

'Oh, they can be perverse,' the Judge says. 'Particularly in motoring cases. Put a dangerous lunatic up and they'll let him off if he can persuade them he's just made an error of judgement, a driving mistake they might have made themselves in an off moment. They think of their precious Minis and Austins and Fords at risk outside the old homestead. Might be nicked any time, mightn't they? They want to hear what young Binder has got to say for himself.'

Without his robes he looks younger and jollier; crisp dark hair springing up on his head and curling thickly on the backs of his otherwise surprisingly delicate hands. He speaks more quickly than he does in court or in the retiring-room and laughs readily, showing large, strong, crooked teeth. A slightly coarse, eager, convivial man, sexually attractive and aware of it, whose healthy brown eyes regard me approvingly. I like the look of him, too, and am amused by the competent speed with which he detached me from my fellow-magistrate, whisking me off to this sheltered corner of the bar the moment Goggle Eyes disappeared to the men's room. I used to wonder how judges could lead an ordinary life. Now I know they take off their robes like actors removing their greasepaint and stepping off stage. I say, smiling at this handsome man, 'They'll let him off, though. I mean, it's so obvious. You think he's innocent, don't you?'

'Probably. Almost certainly, in fact. If I were *quite* certain, you know, I'd have stopped the case, but I don't see how one can be. It's a pretty piddling affair, of course, but it does seem to me that it's up to the jury. I'm a jury man, actually. I know it's fashionable not to be – juries let too many villains off for some people's liking – but you have to weigh the thing up, swings and roundabouts. Why buck the system when you may get something worse in its place?' This is a rhetorical question. He doesn't want a discussion about legal principles with an earnest lady magistrate but a jolly lunch with a pretty woman. He looks at me with his clear, merry gaze and says, 'That's a nice dress you're wearing.'

'It's a suit. A skirt and a jacket.'

'Well, I wouldn't know. Don't know much about women's clothes. Never got married. Never got round to it.' He laughs, as if this is somehow intrinsically comic. 'D'you want to eat now, or would you like another drink first? Long afternoon, I'm afraid. Might as well tank up for it.'

I accept another sherry. I am not hungry, even though I only had orange juice and coffee for breakfast. Sitting opposite Eddie for the last time, I had felt too sick to eat. Eddie had noticed it. Looked up from the detective novel he was reading while he ate eggs and bacon and said, 'You look a bit sickety-poo, pettikins. Sure you're feeling all right?'

His concern was automatic (even before I forced my dry mouth to answer, his eyes had strayed back to his library book), but remembering it constricts my chest now. Indigestion, I tell myself, alcohol on an empty stomach. I smile at the Judge over my fresh drink and say, since a mildly flirtatious response seems expected, 'How did you manage to avoid getting married? It seems a bit ingenuous to say you just never got round to it.'

'A stint at the divorce bar when I was young and impressionable may have put me off. I don't know.'

He gives his sharp, ready laugh. He doesn't look sensitive but perhaps he was once. A young man, sickened by muddle and mess, by the way people who used to love turn on each other.

I say, 'I can see that it might have done. I once gave evidence in a divorce case and it really was very unpleasant.'

I had not expected it to be. Charles was contesting April's application, but I was too amazed at his nerve to be frightened. Sackcloth and ashes should have been Charles's role, in my view! Innocent outrage sustained me as I walked into the witness-box and, telling my story, it seemed clearer than ever that Charles was a monster. I felt almost sorry for his counsel as he stood up and smiled at me. The poor man must feel his task was quite hopeless!

His voice sounded weary as he put his first, gentle questions. He didn't want to make me repeat my evidence in detail. No need to; I had already given it with admirable clarity. There were just one or two points he would like to elucidate. I had come to visit my half-sister and we had been sitting for some time and talking. Where was the baby all this time? In his cot? Yes. Was he sleeping, or restless? Oh, he cried a bit did he? Well, it was time for his feed, of course. As his father had known when he arrived in the flat. Did I really think it was cruel of him to suggest the child might be hungry? Perhaps, since he was a good deal older than his young wife, he was extra conscious of his parental duties. He was a man, after all, who was used to responsibility. A Polish fighter pilot who had fought gallantly for this country during the war and, when it was over, decided to make his home here, start a family. Maybe he was a little irritated, coming home tired after his day's work to find his son crying with hunger and his wife gossiping with her half-sister. The scene that followed had clearly upset me but had it been, really, much more than an ordinary row between husband and wife? Perhaps I couldn't answer that question being unmarried myself. A young, inexperienced girl. The truth is, few marriages are all sun and clear skies and this one – as the husband has freely admitted – was a long way from perfect. But had I ever witnessed any physical violence? Actually seen my brother-in-law strike his wife? Obviously I was concerned when I saw April's bruises, but was that concern a complete explanation for the perhaps slightly *meddlesome* role that I finally played? Removing my sister from her home without telling her husband where she was going? Look at it this way. Two girls the same age; two young sisters. One has got married to an attractive man; the other might be expected to feel – well, a faint jealousy. He wouldn't suggest that this was, in any way, conscious, or that I had set out, deliberately, to make matters worse, but could I be sure, absolutely, that the motives behind what was, from my own evidence, rather high-handed behaviour were totally pure?

This is how I remember my ordeal. It is unlikely, in fact, that Charles's counsel attacked me so crudely. Bullying a witness can be counter-productive. But what he may not have said (or only said through an occasional significant pause, an ironic inflection) my own guilt supplied. As I left the witness-box I was trembling with anger and shame on my own account and apprehension on April's. How could she get her divorce, now my evidence had been so discredited? I was astonished when the Judge granted her decree in a calm, even bored voice; deeply hurt when Steve said, 'Well, Pen, that wasn't too dreadful, was it?' As if what the lawyer had said to me was quite unexceptionable.

He took us out to lunch at the Gay Hussar in Greek Street. April was happy celebrating her freedom. She didn't seem to mind that, although she had care and control of her baby, Charles had been given his custody. Steve said, 'All that solemn guff about his distinguished war-record. I expect that's what did it.'

I said, 'But it's monstrous.' I could not bear to speak of my own humiliation, and this was a useful diversion. 'Charles isn't fit to have custody of a guinea-pig. I should have thought that was obvious – a sadist like that! Though perhaps no one believed he was really so frightful. They didn't seem to believe *me*, anyway!'

I laughed to show this hadn't affected me. Steve said, 'Oh, they did, you know.'

April was reading the menu, murmuring the names of the dishes under her breath like a child learning to read. She had put on weight since she had left Charles and looked smooth and sleek; a tawny young lioness, lazily beautiful. She said, 'Goulash, I think. I need *meat*. But I don't think I can manage three courses. The problem is whether to have something to start with or leave room for pudding.'

Steve said, 'They do a heavenly bortsch soup with sour cream.'

I was afraid I was going to cry. I said, 'You're not really *hungry*?'

Steve said, 'Why not? It's been a long morning.'

April looked sideways at him and giggled. 'Don't be a brute, Steve. That bastard gave her an awful time in the witness-box.'

'Thank you,' I said. 'I'm glad someone noticed.'

Steve smiled at me. 'Come off it, Pen, darling. It's all over now. And you didn't expect him to listen to you in reverent silence, surely? Charles had briefed him. He was only doing his job.'

The easy way he said 'darling' hurt me quite terribly. It meant nothing to him. *I* meant nothing to him – even after all this time I couldn't get used to it! We hadn't seen each other for several months after we ceased to be lovers (although I had telephoned several times, Aunt Madge always answered, and he never replied to my tentative messages), and when we did meet – one Sunday he came home for lunch – he had greeted me with casual affection as if he had never been anything more to me than a kind elder brother. His attitude bewildered and pained, almost frightened me. That anyone could behave as if something had never happened

71

was frightening. I understood, intellectually, that he had simply made up his mind that this was the only way he could deal with the situation, but it seemed cruelly cold to give me no sign, no acknowledgement. I loved him still and asked for so little. Just a silent admission that our love had existed; a smile or a look to show he remembered. Even if he had been stiff with me I could have borne it better than this emotionally aseptic intimacy. This pretence! Perhaps he was more like April than I had ever realised. Like her, he kept his feelings on a tight rein; servants, not masters. Or perhaps neither of them had any really strong feelings at all. April had not appeared even briefly upset during the long morning's hearing. She had given her evidence in a chilly, contemptuous monotone that had seemed to constrain Charles's counsel. Perhaps that was why he had savaged *me*, I thought bitterly. Venting his spleen on an easier victim!

I said, 'All I can say is I'd rather be a dustman than do that kind of job! It seems a disgusting way to earn a living to me. I'd rather be a lavatory attendant. Or sweep streets. At least I'd be cleaning up honest dirt.'

Steve laughed suddenly. 'Or an office cleaner. That's another of the menial tasks you'd be happy to do, isn't it?'

I looked at him, startled. I had offered to get a job as an office cleaner so that we could get married. Had he forgotten? If he had, he remembered now – I saw his teasing expression grow sheepish. I grinned at him with joyful conspiracy. He smiled back, a shy apology, then yelped loudly. April had kicked him under the table.

She said, 'I hope that's ruined his chances of running for England in the next Olympics. I don't know why he's being so bloody smart, Pen. *I'm* sorry you had a rough time, if he isn't. It really was bloody rotten. Have something to eat now and forget all about it.'

At the Gay Hussar we had the bortsch, then the goulash, and drank a dark, heavy Hungarian wine called Bull's Blood. Now, sitting in the dining-room of the Crown Court, we are eating grilled sole on the bone and drinking hock served by the glass.

'Could have been colder,' the Judge says. 'The hock. Otherwise the food isn't bad here, though the helpings are a bit small for my liking.'

He finishes his sole and orders a double portion of treacle pudding. I wonder why I always attract greedy men. It strikes me that when I think of Eddie in future I will see him sitting at table, either in our kitchen at home or in some candle-lit restaurant, cramming food down his gullet, guzzling wine, swilling beer. I have never minded his voracious appetite – it seemed natural in a big man – but it offends me now, suddenly. I remember how he sweats when he eats, mops his damp brow with a large, grubby handkerchief, picks his teeth openly afterwards. Perhaps, subconsciously, I have always been disgusted by his piggish behaviour and am only allowing myself to admit it because I am leaving him. I tell myself this is healthy. To leave someone you have to hate them a little or you will end up hating yourself for what you are doing to them. I cannot really hate Eddie, but in order to cast him off, disentangle myself from the net years of marriage have woven about us, I must make myself hate his faults which are, after all, many and various. It would be insultingly patronising to continue to think of them tenderly. Feeble, false sentiment to pretend I am still 'fond' of Eddie and concerned for his happiness. Rather than fall into that hypocritical trap I had better behave like everyone else when they discard a partner and enumerate his failings, to excuse my own. . . .

The Judge gives a little, pleased sigh as the waitress approaches with his treacle pudding. He picks up his spoon and says, 'My parents were divorced when I was too young to know much about it, but according to my mother's account of her marriage it had been hell on earth. With my father, of course, as chief demon. He seemed decent enough to me whenever I was allowed to see him, but my mother had indoctrinated me so thoroughly that I was almost grown up before I could bring myself to admit that she might have exaggerated her martyrdom. When I did, what you might call my long love affair with my mother was over. I couldn't forgive her for making such a damn fool of me. She used to say the most appalling things about my father. Even though I guessed they were lies, I had to believe them for her sake. And yet she wasn't a wicked woman, y'know, just unhappy and lonely and jealous. Not trained for anything the way women are nowadays, too much time to brood. I was an only child, all she'd got, and she wanted me on her side. Kids do suffer in these situations. I know that's a cliché, but it doesn't make it untrue.'

It seems to me that this disarming confession explains his bachelor state more convincingly than his professional experiences in the divorce court. Although I suspect that laying his cards on the table like this may be his usual approach to women he fancies, I am touched because he is so open about it. I smile sympathetically. 'I suppose a child is always likely to be a bone of contention when parents separate.'

Eddie and I will not fight over our daughters. Even if we wanted to, they are too old to be captured by one side or the other. Too old and too sensible; calm, orderly girls, products of a calm, orderly childhood. I may have failed Eddie but I haven't failed them: they have had love and kindness, good food, dental care, summer camps, bicycles. Their tentative, adolescent rebellions (Louise's untidiness, Jenny's secret smoking and drinking) were dealt with, most of the time, by quietly ignoring them: confrontations, Eddie and I have always agreed, are usually counterproductive. The only time Jenny tried to provoke one, screaming at me, 'I hate you, I really do *hate* you,' because I had told her that even if she wasn't afraid of lung cancer she should know that smoking made her smell like an unemptied ash-tray, I turned the heat off by laughing and saying, 'Do you, darling? Well, there's no need to feel bad about that; it's supposed to be *healthy* to hate your mother!' Now even these minor troubles are over and they are both busy training, Louise to be a speech therapist, Jenny an infant-school teacher. Sensible, secure professions, suited to their not very great talents, and ones they can continue with if they get married and decide to have babies. They belong to the tennis club, attend yoga classes, and Jenny acts in the dramatic society; although she would never be good enough for the professional stage, she has a clear delivery and a 'feel' for character parts. Their lives are purposeful, healthy and full, and the divorce will hardly affect them. Will they blame me? I hope not. I have taught them to be tolerant as I have taught them regular habits and sound ethical principles. The only thing I have failed to teach them, I sometimes think guiltily, is how not to be boring.

The Judge snorts cheerfully. 'Bone of contention is a bit polite, isn't it? A piece of bleeding meat torn apart by two snarling dogs would be rather more accurate.'

He has survived the emotional horrors of his own early life or he could not speak about them so easily, between huge, lusty mouthfuls of treacle pudding, but they are still clearly important to him, part of his assured, solid identity, and this interests me. Perhaps an unhappy childhood does make people more interesting. To me, anyway. Perhaps it is what Louise and Jenny lack in my eyes!

I say, 'I know what you mean. My sister's child was a piece of bleeding meat as you charmingly put it. Not so much when he grew older; his father and mother seemed to lose interest in him once they'd stopped hating each other. But I think all the rows and scenes that went on when he was a little boy have left their mark on him.'

He was such a beautiful baby. A lily-pale, flawless skin, liquid dark eyes and dark hair. A dark Puck, wirily thin and bursting with mischievous energy – once he was walking, it was unsafe to leave him alone for a minute. He was too much for my parents: when April found a part-time job at a local estate agency, I often stayed home and missed lectures. My father objected but, as I told him, April couldn't take time off without getting the sack and I could always borrow another student's notes and write them up in the evenings. Besides, I felt responsible for Adam. He said, 'I know you do, but you aren't. He's April's child, isn't he?'

I tried to explain, one evening when we were washing the supper dishes together, that it was impossible to mark out areas of responsibility in such a crude way. April hated to be tied down; Adam's constant, clamouring demands drove her frantic. It wasn't that she was 'selfish' or 'couldn't be bothered with her own child' as thoughtless people might say. She needed her job and the limited freedom it gave her more than I needed my degree. It was a difference of personality, of basic attitudes, of what we both wanted from life. 'April's Mary, I'm Martha,' I said, wondering if I had got this the right way round and adding, to make myself clear, 'What I enjoy most, and I mean *really* enjoy in the fullest sense, is doing what seems to me the most necessary thing at the moment, whether it's washing the dishes or looking after the baby. It's more important to me than anything I might do in the future if I get my degree. I'm not sacrificing myself! If you like, it's *me* that's the selfish one, doing what *I* want to do, not poor April.'

But he persisted perversely. 'It seems wrong to me. April's made a mess of her life. I don't see why she should expect you to clear it up for her.'

'Because it's better all round. I look after Adam better than she does because I'm more patient, and I get on better with Eve because she feels April despises her.' I lowered my voice, even though the door was closed and Eve had the television on in the sitting-room. 'And I can manage Charles better.'

'Does he need to be managed?' My father stopped drying the plate in his hand and looked at me quizzically.

I tried not to sigh. He was being obtuse to annoy me. Retired men (or so I understood from the psychology lectures that were part of my social studies course) often became quirky and awkward.

I said, 'You know Charles is difficult. But when he comes to see Adam he always behaves better if April's not here. He can't upset *me* – I'm not scared of him, one little bit, and April is, terribly, though she pretends not to be. If he nagged her to let him take Adam out of the house, or even home with him for the night, I'm afraid she'd give in.'

'I don't see why he shouldn't sometimes,' my father said. 'It's his son, isn't it?'

'You *know* why! Please, Daddy, don't be so obstinate. Adam's only little. Charles can't look after him. And there's the very real danger that he might not return him. I think the Judge sensed that. It's why he said that, though Charles should have legal custody, he could only *visit* the child in his mother's home. If *he* didn't trust Charles, why should you? If he did whip Adam off, because he's possessive, or spiteful, or for whatever reason, we might have a hell of a time getting him back. It would mean going to court to get an order or an injunction or something. You know what the Law is like; it might take simply ages – and God knows what would happen in the mind of that baby! He's not a toy for adults to play with but a live human being! It's bad enough when Charles comes to spend an hour or two with him. He's sensitive and he feels the terrible tension. That's why he gets so excited, showing off and screaming with laughter.'

'Is it? Oh, well, if you say so. . . .' My father laughed suddenly. 'There wouldn't be any tension if Charles had the boy to himself, perhaps. Even if he did take him back to his flat, chances are, not that he'd keep him, but that he'd be only too glad to get him back pretty swiftly!'

'We can't risk it!' I cried. The anxiety I felt for Adam was physical: my body ached with it as I rinsed round the sink and wrung out the dishcloth. There were so many dangers! I looked through the window at the dark garden and, for a brief second, thought I saw a face staring in, but it was only my own reflection. I drew the curtains and turned to my father. It was so important to convince him, I thought. I must have an ally. Eve was a broken reed and April, though she was fond of Adam, had in some way moved *on* – marriage and motherhood were behind her and she had set her face to a future that included Adam, of course, but only as an appendage, a relic of her past life to be carried along like an old piece of luggage, dumped in waiting-rooms, left in some attic whenever she wanted to travel free, unencumbered. The sad image brought tears to my eyes. I said urgently, 'You don't understand Charles. He's not like an Englishman, not cool and reasonable. He feels a kind of passionate outrage, as if we'd stolen his baby. *His* son! His *property*! I wouldn't put it past him to do something desperate. Try to sneak Adam out of the country – to the States or somewhere. Charles has a brother in Canada. How would you feel if that happened?'

'I can't think it's likely.' But he sounded doubtful. Doubtful enough, anyway. I shuddered and wept with relief. He put his arms round me. 'There, Pen. Don't cry. There, darling. . . .'

'I love Adam so much. I'm so scared.'

'Yes. I know.'

'*You* love him, don't you? Even if he's not your real grandson, your *blood relation*! In a way, that should make you feel more responsible for him, not less. Shouldn't it?'

'For God's sake, Penelope!' His voice was amused as well as impatient. 'I am devoted to Adam. You know that. Or you ought to. Even if I wasn't, I would, I hope, do my duty. I don't know how I can express it strongly enough to satisfy you. Let's say I'd defend him with my life. Will that do?'

He was laughing openly now. Patting my shoulder and laughing and fishing his handkerchief out of his pocket to dry my hot tears. 'Come on. Blow your nose. There. Is that better?'

'Yes. Thank you, Daddy. I'm sorry.'

'Let's see you smile, then.'

I smiled mournfully. 'I really am sorry. I feel so lonely sometimes. I get stupid.'

'You worry too much about other people's problems. You're too young for it. I don't like to see an old head on young shoulders. I wish. . . .'

He stopped. I looked at him, wondering what he was wishing for me, thinking how comforting it was to have someone care enough to wish *something,* and then, seeing him glance at his watch, blew my nose loudly, a comic exaggeration of a nose-blow to show him he was free now, need not continue with this conversation. My poor father had enough troubles; I mustn't add to them. I said, 'Have I made you miss the news with my silly nonsense? I'm sorry. You'll get the summary at the end, though. Go on in now, and I'll make the coffee.'

I say to the Judge, 'Do you take milk?' The waitress has brought coffee and hot milk in metal pots and turned the handles towards me. I say, 'Seems I'm to be mother.'

'Half and half,' the Judge says. He helps himself to several spoons of sugar.

I say, 'That's a bachelor habit. No nagging woman to tell you to watch your waistline.'

'There are other advantages.' He has, while he ate cheese and biscuits, told me about some of them. He has a flat in the Albany and a housekeeper who comes in by the day but he likes to cook his evening meal for himself, making an event of it, laying the table with candles, listening to music while he eats and settling down to read afterwards. He reads Trollope and Tolstoy, but C. P. Snow is the only modern novelist he appears to have heard of. (He has not heard of Eddie, presumably: our name is so unusual that if he had read Eddie's novel he would almost certainly have enquired if there was a family connection.) The Judge likes, he says, 'the kind of books you can get your teeth into'. He reads novels in this edible category, plays squash twice a week, watches the children's programmes on weekend television and goes to Greece for his holidays. He owns a house in an olive-grove six

miles from Delphi and enjoys being alone there though he sometime invites friends for short periods. Not for too long – 'Fish
and company stink in three days,' he says, and laughs as if he
thinks this remark is original. He stirs his coffee, tastes it, and adds
another heaped spoonful of sugar. He drinks this syrupy sludge,
puts his cup down and says, 'Tell me about your sister's boy. D'you
think he'll come out all right in the end?'

This is a polite social exchange. I have listened to him; it is
my turn to take the floor if I want to. It seems grudging not to
respond, but it isn't easy: Adam's chequered career cannot be
summed up in a few sentences. I honestly believe he is at a turning-
point now, but then I have often honestly believed he was at a
turning-point. When he was six, and April married her solemn
American, a good-tempered, slow-speaking Texan living in
London, I was certain this was the answer to Adam's tantrums and
bed-wetting: a kind stepfather would provide the steadying
influence the poor child had lacked. Disappointed when April
walked out on the marriage after two years and sent Adam to
boarding-school, I rallied fast and decided that this might be, after
all, a better solution: a conventionally structured education away
from his difficult mother could work wonders for an emotionally
troubled, undisciplined boy. I was shocked when he ran away three
years later, taking with him eight pounds stolen from his headmaster's study, glad when he was found a place at a progressive
school where they would encourage his creative talents (at that
time he painted, I thought, most imaginatively), shocked again
when he was expelled at fifteen for smoking pot, but told myself
that if he was taking drugs it was best out in the open at this early
stage when he was clearly only experimenting. I was happy when
he appeared to settle down in a tutorial college in London, living
at home with April and her third husband, a cheerful, expansive
property-dealer, thrilled when he got a Cambridge scholarship, cast
down when he left university halfway through his course to join
a group travelling overland to Australia, delighted when he came

home, a bearded, genial giant with a fillet round his flowing, Old Testament locks, disheartened when it was clear he did not intend to do anything so mundane as earning a living. Now, after several discouraging years, I am beginning to feel hopeful again. Last autumn he was given a suspended prison-sentence for peddling cannabis and, although hope is not the obvious response to this situation, I am sure the shock has been salutary. And his girl-friend Elvira is pregnant. She is no match for Adam, a pale, dreary young woman with about as much life in her as a stick of limp celery, but her coming child may be his salvation. Even if he does not care how he lives for himself, he will not want to bring up his baby on social-security handouts. 'Elvira can get a job, can't she? I believe in sex equality, equal rights, equal duties,' he said when I put this to him but he was only teasing. He had dressed in a suit to lunch with me in London, and when I complimented him on his appearance he said he had decided to join the Establishment. Not the Civil Service, of course, or anything *boring,* but he would quite like, he said, an interesting job in publishing. His tone was youthfully pompous but his eyes were anxious and vulnerable.

I say to the Judge, 'He's still very vulnerable.'

When I look at Adam I see a frightened little boy, screaming.

He was two years old. Eve was in hospital again for a course of electro-convulsive therapy. I had been to visit her while Adam was tucked up for his afternoon nap. I came home to find Charles's old car parked at the gate. Anger made my mind race as I ran up the little path and fumbled for my key. How dare Charles arrive like this, unexpectedly, without warning. He was supposed to telephone first, wasn't he? I flung the door open, ready for battle. Charles, standing in the hall, turned and observed me indifferently as if I were a cat or a dog walking in. My father said, 'Pen. . . .' in a quavery, old man's voice. He was halfway up the stairs, blocking them, one hand on the wall, the other on the banister-rail.

Charles ignored me and shouted at him, 'It is my right to see my son. You cannot stop me. '

Adam said, 'My daddy. My daddy come.' I looked up and saw him on the landing. Quarrelling voices had woken him; he was pale and shivering, plastic pants dangling awkwardly between his bare legs. He was clutching his teddy bear.

I said softly, 'Please don't frighten him, Charles.'

'Go to hell.' Charles's smooth, waxy skin was a darker colour than usual. Temper had darkened it. He started up the stairs. My father said, 'No. . . .' Charles tried to push past him, striking his hand from the banister, and the old man gave a gasp and lurched sideways. I ran forward and he toppled towards me, crumpling at the knees, eyes rolling upwards. I tried to break his fall but he was too heavy; he collapsed against me like a sack of potatoes and we tottered together across the hall, knocking over a table. A glass bowl of flowers fell and shattered. My father lay on the ground on his back, surrounded by wicked splinters of glass and small pink-and-white flowers, like confetti. I slipped in a patch of water and sat down with a jarring thump. There was a sharp pain in my hand. I saw the blood ooze along the line of the gash like a string of small garnets. I crawled on my hands and knees to my father.

I said, 'Daddy.' And cradled his dead head in my lap.

I said to Eve afterwards, 'He died in my arms.' I suppose I thought this might comfort her. In fact he had suffered a massive heart-attack; had died as he fell. 'The old pump gave out at last' was how his doctor explained it. He was a bluff man, given to homely analogies. 'I warned him to take better care of his ticker,' he told me later that afternoon, 'but I don't think he paid much attention.'

At the time all I knew was that my father's face was a dark lilac colour except for a patch of white, flabby skin round his mouth, and that there was blood on his shirt from my hand which was now bleeding freely. Blood everywhere – and the child screaming desperately. The sound hammered my ears. I cried out, 'All right,

Adam, I'm coming.' Charles was kneeling beside me, loosening my father's collar, lifting his head from my lap. I stumbled to my feet and ran up the stairs. The little boy shrank away from me, hitting out with his teddy bear, red face contorted. I said, 'Adam, darling,' but he turned and ran, plastic pants squelching, across the landing and into the bathroom. He slammed the door in my face and shot the bolt. I rattled the door knob. 'Let me in, sweetheart. Let Auntie Pen in.' But he was wailing too loud to hear me. Weeping myself, I thumped with my bloody hand on the door. Charles was shouting. He was on the landing, catching hold of my wrists, mopping my cut hand with his handkerchief. He made a pad of it, pressing it into my palm. 'Hold it there. We will clean the cut later.' I moaned, '*Adam*,' and he said, 'He's all right for a minute. Please be brave. Listen. Your father is dead, I think. We must telephone for his doctor.' I stared at him, shocked into silence. His full cheeks were pale now, his round, polished eyes grave. A blue vein I had never noticed before pulsed in his temple. He said, 'I'm so sorry,' put his arms round me and held me against him. His damp mouth was close to my ear. He was sweating. I smelled his sweat, felt the firmness and warmth of his stomach, and was suddenly seized with such sharp sexual hunger that for a moment it took me over completely. Sagging in his arms, limp and moist with desire, I saw myself lying beneath him, legs spread wide on the carpeted landing, or pressed against the bolted door behind which his child was still crying, though less urgently now. Perhaps he would cry himself to sleep, I thought crazily, and give me a chance to make love with his father. I chuckled deep in my throat, as I huddled close, my breasts tingling. His embrace tightened briefly, then he gave a short, strangled laugh and released me. He said, 'Not quite the moment, I think,' and I was overtaken with shame, leaning against the wall with closed eyes to shut out the sight of his cold, laughing face, sobbing with adventitious hysteria to cover up this dreadful indignity. Should I scream? Faint? I knuckled my fists into my eyes like a child and gasped, between sobs, 'He's not dead. He can't be. If he is dead, you killed him. Oh, my daddy, my daddy.'

Charles slapped my face, not hard but noisily, with his cupped hand. When I looked at him, I saw his eyes glistening. He said, 'Do you want me? Well, you can't have me. Go to the telephone. I will see to the boy.'

He pushed me towards the stairs and stood by the bathroom door. 'Adam. Listen to me. Get up off the floor and pull back the bolt. Let me come in. Do as I tell you or I will be angry.'

Excitement stirs in me now as I remember that scene. I remember my father's death in my mind, with pity and sadness, but I remember Charles with my body.

I look at the Judge and shiver with secret, physical pleasure as I realise that he attracts me as Charles did. They are both competent, authoritative men, perhaps slightly contemptuous of women. Why should this excite me? Do I find it a challenge? Oh, of course not. What rubbish! If I wanted Charles, it was only because he was Adam's father. It was Adam I loved, yearning over him with a passion that made my conscientious affection for my own babies such a disappointing, thin-blooded business: looking into their plump, sweet, anxious faces I longed for a dark, fiercer spirit. I am ashamed of this disloyalty, naturally. Or had been ashamed of it once.

I say, 'Adam's father is what is called a "strong" character. An old-fashioned, masculine man, a bit of a brute in a way. That's hard on a boy if he feels he can't measure up.'

'Do you like brutish men?' the Judge asks, smiling suddenly.

'Of course not,' I cry, shocked by this dreadful suggestion.

The Judge laughs. 'No need to be so indignant. You know, the English are a violent people at bottom. It's why we always reject the idea of violence so furiously. Sometimes I think it's why we have such respect for the law. More respect than most nations. We know it keeps our instincts for looting and raping in check.'

'I'm a violent woman, am I? Is that what you mean?' I feel oddly flattered – for 'violent' read 'passionate' – and the Judge knows it. He doesn't answer directly but watches me with bright, amused eyes as he dabs his full mouth with his napkin and pushes his chair back. He looks at his watch and sighs lightly: all good things come to an end. He says, 'We've got about twenty minutes. I expect you have a few things to do.'

There are two telephone calls I must make before the court sits again. One is necessary, the other an important indulgence. But I am reluctant to end this comfortable interlude. I murmur, 'Of course one always thinks one is so controlled and logical. I had an anonymous letter the other day. Now, you'd think that wouldn't really disturb me, or not after the first stupid shock, but I can't put it out of my mind. I keep coming back to it.' I explain about the aspirins in the brown envelope, my name and address in scarlet block capitals, and the Judge listens, frowning. He says slowly, 'How very unpleasant for you.'

'Yes. I suppose so.' I laugh with a faint, nervous tremor. 'Though daft to brood about it perhaps.'

He looks at me thoughtfully. 'Any idea where it came from? Anyone who might have it in for you?'

'I can't think. It doesn't *matter*. Only makes me uncomfortable. As if I'd been accused of some secret depravity. I don't know what I've been accused *of*; that's really the trouble. Does that seem silly?'

'No. However clear one's conscience, it's never clear enough, is it?'

I am amazed that he understands this. I feel lightened and eased by his understanding; grateful to this sympathetic, solid, dependable man. I say, handing over my burden, 'There's nothing I can do about it, of course.'

'It could be investigated. Though it's probably not worth it unless something similar happens again. Or has happened before. It hasn't, I take it?'

I shake my head, smiling.

'No, of course not. You'd have done something about it, like a sensible woman. Perhaps you should now. I'm not sure. I'll think about it.'

'Please don't. There's no need. It's enormously kind of you just to have listened.'

'Nonsense.' He hesitates, then touches my hand with his hairy, delicate fingers – a brief, darting gesture, unexpectedly awkward and shy. Perhaps he is shy beneath that confident manner, I think as I retreat to the washroom and, regarding my flushed face in the mirror, recognise that I find this idea mildly titillating. I smile at myself as I wash my hands and arrange my hair and put on fresh lipstick. My reflection is more reassuring than it was several years ago, before I began to need glasses for reading, and although I know that if I were to put them on now to make up my face, the pouches and wrinkles would leap into focus, I prefer to accept the comforting bonus the years have provided. After all, if I look prettier to myself now my sight has deteriorated, I presumably look prettier to others in the same boat. The Judge may be slightly younger than I am, and I cannot remember if he wore glasses to read the court papers this morning, but his eyes are unlikely to be as sharp as they used to be. Certainly it is pleasanter to assume that when he looks at me he sees what I see when I look in the mirror. Illusion is good for the spirits; it may even improve the reality. As I formulate this neat thought I am reminded of my little stepmother. When my father died, she moved into a small flat in London, had pink-tinted mirrors installed in her bedroom and bathroom, and from that moment her frail beauty flowered like a late autumn rose.

And not only her beauty. Her personality changed within a few months, blossomed miraculously into a sturdy independence that astonished us all. She bought herself fashionable clothes, had her hair dyed, found a job as a dentist's receptionist. She looked a new woman and became a new woman. It was as if, though she grieved for my father, his death had released her from some kind of bondage. 'She always felt she'd let him down' was Steve's explanation. 'And not only him. You, me and April too. It was too much to bear, so she escaped into illness.'

'She never let *me* down,' I protested.

'Well, she felt that she did. Your dad away fighting for his country, and she couldn't even take care of his child. Though perhaps it isn't so simple. I think she never really got over the feeling that she'd done a wicked thing, getting divorced and remarried. She was a very conventional woman, and her family blamed her. Her parents never spoke to her again, did you know that? They *died* without seeing her! Perhaps she felt, all the time your father was alive, that she was really living in sin.'

'How ridiculous. Steve, you are being ridiculous.'

'I'm sure I am, darling, but people's *lives* are often ridiculous, aren't they?'

When had this conversation taken place? Frowning at my reflection, my face seems to grow younger and rounder. I remember a dark saloon bar. Red cushions on reproduction-oak settles and something about the occasion, some tension. The air was charged with it, like summer thunder. There was sweat on Steve's hawkish nose, sweat darkening his fair, crinkly hair. We were discussing Eve – but we hadn't met for that purpose, surely? No, of course not. I had asked him to meet me – at this time we never met casually – to tell him I was marrying Eddie.

It took me some time to get round to it. We talked about Eve, about the Government's ridiculous Suez adventure, and about April, who had just met her Texan. I told Steve how much I hoped April would marry this good American. He would be a steadying influence on her and an excellent father for Adam. Steve listened and nodded but interrupted before I had finished telling him how important this marriage might be for our nephew, to ask how I was. 'I mean, how are you *really*?' he asked, with one of his sweet, frowningly serious looks, and it suddenly struck me that the reason he had come here this evening, why he always came now whenever I wanted to see him, was because my father was dead and he thought he should keep an eye on me, take on his responsibilities as head of the family. This amused me – it was so typical of Steve, so chivalrous and old-fashioned – but it hurt and saddened me too. Was this all I meant to him? Just another one of his duties? I told him more curtly than I had meant to that I was very happy and that I was marrying Eddie. Eddie was a marvellous man and a marvellous writer. Even Steve, who never seemed to read anything for pleasure except *The Decline and Fall of the Roman Empire*, must have heard of Eddie's famous war-novel, *X, Y, and Zed*. It had been a bestseller both in England and in America. Eddie was very modest about his success. He had not mentioned his book until he asked me to marry him. He said he thought I ought to know he had written it – as if it were a skeleton that might otherwise tumble out of a cupboard sometime and frighten me. I had met Eddie in the mental hospital shortly after my father died, one afternoon when I was visiting Eve and Eddie was visiting his ex-wife who was a patient on the same ward. We had known each other for eighteen months, and last week I had said I would marry him.

And now I am leaving him. I have washed my hands and combed my hair and retired to the chaste privacy of the lady magistrates' rest-room to make my two telephone calls. Sitting at the writing-table that holds the telephone, a tortoiseshell tray containing an assortment of felt-tipped pens and a leather-framed blotter, I feel a sudden exhaustion, a tremendous, paralysing lassitude as if I had been toiling for hours up a steep mountain and collapsed just short of the summit, legs too weak to carry me further. I yawn hugely, shoulders sagging, eyelids leadenly drooping. I haven't the energy to pick up the receiver, dial a number. Although I have travelled so far already, prepared myself for this journey not only morally but practically – sorted my clothes, left Eddie's all washed and mended, stocked up the deep freeze and larder, paid the household bills up to date – I am too weary to take this last step. And yet I must take it; there is nothing else I can do, no decent alternative. The situation I am in does not admit compromise and I know it. I have lain awake night after night, arguing with myself, presenting my case as objectively as I can, trying to see how it might appear to others and deciding, in the end, that how it appears to me is what matters.

I say aloud, 'Action Stations!' And pull a wry face: this is what Eddie says when he drags himself out of his normal lethargy – out of his bath, his armchair, his bed – to perform some small, tiresome task. Perhaps his vast idleness is contagious and over the years I have caught it? I puff out my cheeks, laughing self-consciously, pick up the telephone and begin to dial – for some reason clumsily using one of the felt-tipped pens for this purpose – and stop. I will make the inessential call first. Is this weakness? Perhaps. But leaving Eddie is the first really hard thing I have had to do in my whole life and I must limber up for it. I may have thought I made choices before, hesitating conscientiously between one course and another, honestly and honourably concerned to take the right one, but all those anxious, interior monologues now seem little more than play-acting. Amateur theatricals indulgently watched by kind friends from the stalls.

Looked at this way, speaking to Desdemona will be quite a tough kind of rehearsal. Though she is, strictly speaking, a friend, she is neither indulgent nor kind and I am, to be truthful, slightly afraid of her. Partly because she is lesbian, and partly because she is so successful professionally. A junior editor when Eddie's novel came out, she is now a director of the same publishing house. Suitably placed, in fact, to help Adam acquire his 'interesting' job (which is, of course, why I am telephoning), though whether she will actually do so is questionable. I am not so besotted as to be blind to Adam's lack of achievement, his almost total absence of qualifications. His charms will hardly seduce Desdemona. On the other hand, since she is a fair-minded woman she might lean over backwards not to be prejudiced against him on that very account. Hard to say. Listening to the telephone ring, I use a green felt-tipped pen to draw a small, peacock-like bird in one corner of the white, virgin blotter, and wonder vaguely about sexual attitudes. Absurd that I should be nervous of Desdemona when I enjoy, as most women do, the company of male homosexuals. They present, presumably, no physical threat. Do hetero men like lesbians for the same reason? Certainly Eddie and Desdemona are always comfortable together. They both like substantial meals and malt whisky, and they are both heavy smokers. A picture of Desdemona, glass in hand, cigar-ash on the soft shelf of her bosom, floats into my mental vision in the same moment that she answers the telephone. Her cool, light, girlish voice makes her sound younger than she is, which is roughly my age.

I say, 'Des. It's Penelope. Have you taken over the switchboard as well as everything else?' And laugh awkwardly in case Desdemona should think I am accusing her of being aggressive, unfeminine.

'One of the girls is out at lunch, the other off sick. I switched the beastly thing through. You're ringing about Adam, I take it?'

'I'm afraid so. Sorry, Des.' Why should I be *sorry*?

'Why sorry?'

'Well. Taking your time up with my wretched nephew. Has he written?'

'Yes. Did you think he wouldn't? He wrote an astonishingly *good* letter as a matter of fact.' She chuckles with what seems surprise. 'Hang on a minute, I'll find it.' A rustle of papers. Desdemona's desk is always a muddle. Not her mind, though. Did that chuckle mean she has guessed that I drafted Adam's 'good' letter? I resign myself to hearing my own well-thought-out phrases repeated to me and resist a faint sense of disquiet. Does it matter if Desdemona finds it amusing to tease me? At least Adam typed out the letter himself, took the trouble to sign it, stamp it and post it. If he wasn't really keen he wouldn't – on previous form – have bothered to do even that.

Desdemona says, 'Never mind now. It'll turn up. I was quite impressed, if that comforts you. Enough to see him, anyway. Can't promise anything, as you must know, of course. We're firing, not hiring, at present. It depends what his expectations are.'

'Humble, I think.' I tell this brazen lie cheerfully, brushing aside the memory of Adam's graciously condescending agreement when I offered to speak to Eddie's publishers on his behalf, his smiling assertion that he would only consider something 'really creative'. He won't dare take that line with Desdemona, surely? The important thing is to get him an interview. I say, 'Of course he's *hopeful* like all the young nowadays. His generation simply isn't scared of unemployment the way we were brought up to be. I don't suppose he'll grovel exactly, but he really is anxious to get a toe-hold in publishing, and I think you'll find he's quite realistic.'

'His letter struck just that note,' Desdemona says. 'Just the right balance between ambition and modesty.'

'Did it? I'm glad.' My heart thumps uncomfortably. I give a light laugh. 'I'm prejudiced, naturally, being so fond of him. But even *objectively* I think he really is clever. It's just taken him time to find out what he wants to be clever *at*.' I wonder if I should tell Desdemona why he left Cambridge and decide it would be pushing my luck to explain that he felt the Classical Tripos was 'dead and irrelevant'. I say, 'Of course, now he's decided, he's just like any other young man in a hurry. And I think the bit of trouble I told you about, this drugs charge, means he's likely to be rather more serious. He really does need a job, Des.'

'So do a lot of people,' Desdemona says dryly. And, ending this conversation, 'How's Eddie?'

'Well. *Actually.*' I moisten my lips, pick up another felt pen and stab at the peacock bird, giving him a red eye. 'That's another thing. I'm leaving him.' I am astonished that I find this so easy to say. 'You're the first person I've told, actually. I'm leaving it to him to tell most of our friends. It seemed fairer. But I thought it might help if you knew. He's fond of you. And you live close enough. Our side of London. I don't mean I want you to go and do anything for him. Just that he'd feel it wasn't an imposition to ask you.'

There is a pause. Desdemona is digesting this information. Or perhaps she is lighting a cigar. Eventually she says, 'I'm sorry. How does he feel about it?'

'I don't know. I haven't told him. I didn't want a scene and I thought he wouldn't, either. You know how he always cries. It would be so humiliating for him.'

Desdemona says, with a smile in her voice, 'Do you think so? Men always used to cry. In Elizabethan times it was considered manly.'

Well, I can't bear it when he does. So I left him a note.'

'On the pillow? A pincushion?' Desdemona's voice sharpens.

'No. In his typewriter. Under the cover. I didn't want him to know until later. Until I was on my way, so to speak. And I know bloody well he won't start working before the late afternoon if I'm out of the house. Lazy bugger.'

'Slave-driver,' Desdemona counters. And laughs.

I have faced this accusation too often in my own mind to be more than mildly irritated. 'Not a very successful one, it would seem. Oh, I know he works on the telly plays, bashing them out when he has a deadline, and I don't despise them, you know bloody well I don't. After all, more people see one of those plays in an evening than will ever read his book in a lifetime. But he hasn't touched the new novel for God knows how long. There's a block somewhere. To tell you the truth, I'm beginning to feel *I'm* the block. He may be able to get on with it once I'm gone. It's not *why* I'm going, and I wasn't going to mention it – too much like the ghastly special pleading couples always go in for when they break up but it may just be true in this case. I'm a stronger character than he is, but he's stubborn, and this is the only way he can fight me. Show me where I get off! "This is one thing you *can't* make me do" – that's what he's saying!'

Desdemona does not reply. She has the disconcerting habit of remaining silent when something – even if only a formal answering murmur of assent or negation – seems called for. I remind myself that her silence does not necessarily mean disapproval, simply that she has, at the moment, no useful comment to make. All the same, it makes me uneasy. Desdemona often makes me uneasy – and garrulous. I say, with a foolish, forced giggle, 'I expect too much of him, maybe. Or he thinks I do. He thinks *I* think: Here is this genius! Why doesn't he get on with it and show us what he can do! And you can't say to him that it's not what you think because just denying it implies that you *do*! To some extent, anyway. It's like asking, Have you stopped beating your wife yet? On the other hand, it may not be anything to do with it. I mean, *I* may not be. Perhaps it's self-regarding to think so. Eddie may just be a one-book man. That's not unheard of, is it? How many years since *X, Y and Zed,* after all? Nearly twenty! Any publisher who expected a follow-up must have given up all hope by now.'

'Oh, one never gives up hope,' Desdemona says. 'Look. I'll ring him this evening. Go and get drunk with him, if you think that would help. Or if it seems that he wants me to.'

Her cool acceptance of the situation is a little discomfiting. A normal woman would want to know more. Am I leaving Eddie for someone else? Or am I just clearing out? Not that I want to be asked – or to answer – such questions. Indeed, knowing Desdemona won't pry is why I have told her. Or is this one of the reasons.

'I say, 'Thank you, Des. I really do thank you for listening. It seems drearily phony to say I'm concerned about Eddie, but knowing you know what has happened and will stretch out a hand if he needs it is such a comfort to me, if only a selfish one. Easing *my* conscience! But it will help him, too! You can help him – and not just through this bad patch. You're his publisher. I know you've never bullied him over the novel, but perhaps it's about time you did!' I try to speak lightly and humorously: although I have often felt Desdemona should try a bit harder with Eddie, take his talent more seriously, I don't want to appear critical of her professional competence. 'I'm sorry to go on about it. But it seems such a waste. He *can* do it. Why doesn't he?'

'Perhaps he is waiting for Estelle to die.' Desdemona says this so calmly that it takes several seconds for her words to sink in. When they do, I feel a physical shock – as if I have been thumped hard in the stomach. I know why Desdemona never asks 'ordinary' questions. It is not because she is a lesbian and therefore lacks natural feminine curiosity but because she knows all the answers.

Estelle is Eddie's first wife. He met her on the cross-Channel boat just after the war; a crowded, rough, uncomfortable passage from Ostend to Dover. Eddie's short sight had kept him out of the Services; he had spent his war in the Ministry of Information and was, at this time, working in Paris. He was going home because his mother was dying. Thinking about her he was less self-conscious and so less shy than usual. When he saw a tear-stained young woman struggling up the gangway with a heavy suitcase, he lumbered forward to help her without hesitation. He found her a seat in the bar, bought her a brandy. His kindness made her tears flow. She had just been to her husband's funeral, which had taken place near Paris in somewhat odd circumstances.

Estelle was French. She had married an Englishman, a wine-shipper, in the late thirties. During the war, this man (Zed in the novel) had been recruited into the Special Operations Executive and, with two other agents, X and Y, was dropped in France six weeks before D-Day. They were to blow up a couple of bridges and prepare the local Resistance for the Allied landing. Nothing was heard from them; the mission was never accomplished. When the European war ended, X and Y turned up in London. They had returned separate ways and they told different stories. X said that Zed had lost his nerve and refused to carry out his instructions; Y that he had betrayed them to the Gestapo. Both insisted that they had been lucky to escape with their lives. They did not know what had happened to Zed. No one, apparently, questioned their statements and no investigation was ordered. More than a year later (a few weeks before this boat journey) an army major, travelling through the area where X, Y and Zed had been operating, stopped in a village and was told by a farmer that there was the body of a British agent down a dry well on his land. The man had been murdered, the farmer said. He didn't know why, or by whom; such things happened in wartime, and wise people did not pry or pass judgement. But, since the war was now over, he would be grateful if the British would remove their dead man from his well.

The documents found on the body were false, but there was a snapshot of Estelle among them. This was returned to her, as was the watch and the cuff-links that Zed had been wearing. His body was taken to Paris and buried, and the British embassy had sent a member of their staff to the funeral. This diplomatic action bore out, Estelle said, that British Intelligence knew perfectly well what she had always known: that her husband had been not a coward, but a hero. X and Y had been the cowards – and the villains. They had killed Zed because they had been afraid to obey his orders. It was clear that Intelligence understood what had happened and equally clear that they intended to do nothing about it. No action would be taken, either to accuse X and Y, or to remove the slur from her husband. Inertia, perhaps, was responsible; her own view was that X and Y had friends to protect them. 'I expect,' she said bitterly, 'that they were at school with someone or other.'

Eddie had six weeks' leave. He buried his mother, wrote the best part of his novel, and fell in love with Estelle. His love for her fired him; her outraged defence of her husband seemed a brave, beautiful thing. The story soared on the wings of his love into high, dramatic romance: the tale of a faithful widow, battling against the indifference of bureaucracy and conspiracy in high places to vindicate her dead husband's memory. He wrote at speed, with passion, and with knowledge culled from his years in the Ministry, of the incompetence and deceit with which the secret affairs of state are often conducted. He showed it, when it was finished, to a friend who had an uncle who was a publisher.

He was shy of showing the book to Estelle. They were already married when the advance copies came. He had dedicated it to her, a lover's gift, like a ring or a rose. She read it and said nothing, though he thought she looked at him strangely. He was disappointed but assumed, humbly, that his small offering was simply not good enough and she preferred a kind silence to criticism. Six months later, when the book was on its third printing, she turned on him like a tiger. She had kept her mouth shut up to now, expecting – and hoping – that the novel would drop into decent oblivion, but she couldn't keep quiet any longer. What Eddie had done was quite unendurable. He had taken her story – her *life* – and perverted it. He had turned her into a romantic dupe, made it clear that, although she was too stupid to see it, her husband had been a coward and a traitor. Eddie reread his book and saw this was true: writing as he had done, through Estelle's eyes, he had turned Zed into an impossible hero. At the same time he could not help recognising that this point of view was to a large extent responsible for the success of the story: the widow's blind belief gave it a tragic depth that was all the more poignant because, as he wrote, he had believed that he shared it. The irony shocked and appalled him. He protested his innocence, but Estelle said he could never have produced this effect if he had not believed Zed was guilty. Eddie searched his heart and decided that she was probably right and for a most shameful reason: he was jealous of Zed and had meant to defame him. How could he compete, after

96

all, with a dead hero? He confessed and wept. Estelle made it clear she despised him. He begged her forgiveness, and she said he would never have it as long as she lived. He was a thief – he had stolen her husband's good name, blazoned his guilt abroad. He might just as well have murdered him. No doubt he would be glad to see her dead too. She had served her purpose now he had written his novel. If she had not been his wife, she could have gone to law, forced him to retract his libel, made him pay for it. He had only married her to prevent her exposing him as a liar, a falsifier. She raged on like this for weeks, gave him no rest, woke him up at night to revile him. She accused him of wishing her dead, then of actually trying to kill her. She refused to eat food he prepared, to take drink from his hand. His shame and remorse were too great for him to see what was happening. Although she ranted on like a mad woman, he did not see she was mad. One evening he found her pounding up an empty scent-bottle with a hammer. 'Ground glass in my soup,' she cried. 'I know what you're doing.' He wrenched the hammer away and she grabbed a jagged splinter of glass and backed round the table, her eyes pale and crazily flickering. Her tongue flicked in and out of her mouth like a snake's tongue as she shouted insults at him. He was afraid to go near her. She slashed her wrists as he watched, screamed round the flat dripping blood while he called the ambulance, cowered in a corner when the men came to fetch her, spitting like a wild cat, tearing her hair out in handfuls.

Grief and guilt filled his days. He was convinced he had driven her mad, that some darkness in him had infected her. When she recovered enough to file divorce papers he did not try to prevent her. Once she was rid of him, the source of her illness, the disease-carrier, the shadow might lift from her mind. He did not see her for several months after the decree was made absolute, then heard she was ill again. She had tried to strangle herself with the lavatory chain. A man from the electricity company came to read the meter, heard her terrible, gurgling cries through the door and broke into the flat. Eddie went to the hospital, saw the dreadful marks on her throat and blamed himself for not keeping in touch with her. No one else cared, it seemed. Her family lived in France and though, when she married Eddie, she had been on good terms with Zed's family, she had, as time passed, ceased to see them. She said to Eddie, 'So you've come at last, have you?' with an air of sly triumph. Nothing more. She turned over in bed and lay with her back to him for the rest of his visit – but when he had gone she 'perked up', so the staff told him the next time he came, and regaled the ward with lively accounts of his wicked attacks on her. She was insanely obsessed, but her obsession was all the life left to her; without it, she was little more than a vegetable.

Eddie continued to visit her in the mental hospital, which was where I first met him. I was visiting Eve, and Estelle was one of a group playing cards in the day room. Her stubby fingers dealing the cards had ridged, bitten nails. She was a loony, a nut; a short, shapeless woman with greying, cropped hair and grey, flickering eyes. Eve said Estelle believed her husband was trying to kill her. She believed that was why she was in the hospital. Estelle told everyone this. She said, 'He can't get at me here. They let him come to see me otherwise he might run wild and kill other people.'

'Why *do* you go?' I asked Eddie when he told me the truth. Or what he knew of it.

He had just asked me to marry him. We were sitting in his car outside the house in Putney where I had rented a room ever since Eve sold up and moved into London.

'I'm ashamed,' he said, and wept. I had never seen a man cry like this before, with such damp, total abandon, and sat, deeply embarrassed, while he leaned his head on his hands, on the steering-wheel, his whole body heaving and shaking. His heavy shoulders shook under his heavy tweed jacket.

After a while, I touched his arm cautiously. He sat up and blew his nose, trumpeting loudly into a huge crimson handkerchief. He blinked as approaching headlights splashed like soft exploding gold flowers on the windscreen, and I saw the tears on his cheeks. He mopped them up, dabbed at his pale, freckled forehead, smoothed back his limp, sparse, ginger hair. He said, 'Sorry. I'm strung up. Getting out that proposal and being accepted. You did say yes, my lamb, didn't you? I didn't dream it? Too much excitement, tears before nightfall, as Nanny would say. Forgive me, my preciouskins. About Estelle. She's a paranoid schizophrenic. It's not supposed to be my fault, but I feel that it is. *I* wrote that bloody book! *I* married her!' He paused and gave a long, shuddering sigh. 'I don't think,' he said miserably, 'I was a very competent lover.'

He looked at me shyly. We had known each other for eighteen months, been to the cinema and the theatre together, eaten a great many large meals in expensive restaurants. I had been astonished at the amount of money he had spent on me and how little he asked in return. He had kissed me good night, sighing tenderly, calling me his baby, his angel-pie; held my hand, stroking my palm with his finger; touched my breasts very occasionally. That was all. I had thought he did not want to make love to me; now I saw he had simply been frightened. I was embarrassed, and moved. He was older than I was, a successful writer, a rich man. The only child in a rich, sterile family, he had inherited from his mother, his father, and would inherit more when his maiden aunts died. There was something tremendously, wonderfully touching about this big, rich, powerful man weeping so humbly in front of me, being so frightened. The thought that I could, perhaps, do something for him excited me. I was sure I could help him! He probably saw sex as a challenge, saw his penis as a lance with which he must conquer the world. I had read somewhere (at this time most of what I knew about life came from books) that some men suffered from this grotesque expectation. Poor Eddie! Had his lunatic wife taunted him? *I* would comfort him, show him there need be no dreadful complexities. Foolish people created complexities by expecting too much from what should be a simple, warm, human act in which friendship and being at ease with each other were really more important than love. Steve had loved me, and left me. There had been two men since then, two fellow-students, but they had been brief affairs and although I had been happy in bed with them I could barely remember their faces. I hadn't loved them. Did I love Eddie? I must love him a little, since I had said I would marry him. Not as I loved Steve, of course, but that had been *agony*. This was something deeper, more lasting. I felt tenderness for Eddie, a soft, tender pity that committed me to him. He really did need me and I was so proud to be needed.

I said, 'Darling Eddie, it'll be all right for us. Don't worry. Just trust me. Everything will be all right, I promise you.'

Sitting on a reproduction-oak settle in the dark bar, I said to Steve, 'Eddie needs me. That's very important.'

'Do you need *him*, though?' Steve's voice was husky. He cleared his throat and laughed. 'I mean, do you love him?'

I couldn't see his face clearly but he sounded cheerful and that made me angry. I had meant to say something loving; tell him, perhaps, as a kind of sentimental farewell, that I loved Eddie differently from the way I'd loved him (the way I *still* loved him, I had meant to say, if he pressed me); but the feeling that he had only come here this evening as a family duty made me angry with him.

I said, 'You don't sound very pleased. It's not very nice of you. Aren't you pleased for me, Steve?'

He reached out and patted my hand. A condescending gesture, I thought, as if my hand were a cat or a dog sitting next to him. 'Of course, darling. I'm pleased if you're really happy. But you keep tellling me how much Eddie needs you. As if you thought that was what really mattered. I don't feel like crippling myself falling over with pleasure because you're marrying someone richer than me, more successful, in every way more desirable, just because he apparently *needs* you. Why are you sorry for him, anyway? This gloomy Rochester figure with a lunatic wife gibbering away in the nut-house. Is that *why*? Do you think it's so wildly romantic?'

'Don't be foul.'

'I'm just interested.'

'No, you're not. You're just scoring points. Eddie being richer than you is nothing to do with it, unless you're just jealous.'

'Why should I be jealous?'

'No reason. No reason at all.' I felt myself blushing with shame and was glad it was so dark in the bar. I said quickly, 'Why shouldn't I be sorry for poor Eddie, anyway? He's had a rotten time. Having a wife go mad and feeling it's in some way your fault isn't *funny*. You ought to know that. You of all people! You didn't think it was so terribly comic when your mother went off her head. Did you, Steve?'

'Shut up,' he said. 'Shut up, Pen.'

'All right. But stop making mean, silly jokes.'

'I didn't mean to. I'm just bothered by your attitude. It seems so important to you, psychologically, to be sorry for this man you're going to marry, and that seems all wrong to me.'

'Not to me, though! If it's psychologically important to me, as you put it, to think I can do something for someone, why is that wrong?'

'I can think of better reasons for getting married. Does it embarrass you to tell me you love him? Or do you really fancy yourself with a martyr's crown? They can be awfully prickly. Does Eddie still see Estelle? Does he still love her?'

'I don't know. I don't *ask*. I wouldn't grudge it to her anyway. That poor woman. If Eddie's still a bit fond of her I'm glad about it. She has so little, why should I want to take that little away from her? Jealousy is so vile. I wish I'd not told you, Steve. I wish I'd just got married and then told you after. Then you wouldn't have picked me to pieces like this, as if I were a child, or a stupid adolescent girl anyway, who had no idea what she was doing. It's cruel of you, Steve.'

He was silent a minute. Then he said, rather distantly, 'I'm sorry. I didn't mean to be cruel. But you shouldn't lose your temper because I ask you quite ordinary questions.'

I said angrily, 'They're not ordinary questions and you've no right to ask them. But I'll answer you. Of course I love Eddie. I love him enormously. He's a marvellous man, kind and good and wonderfully talented and terribly funny and sweet. I just don't rate myself so highly that I think my loving him is *enough*. It wasn't enough for *you*, after all. So I need to feel I can do something more for him if I'm going to be a good wife. It's a comfort to *me* to think I can be a real comfort to him. That's why I keep on about how he needs me, not because it means I don't love him. I can do things for him and I'm glad there are things to be done. I can help him with Estelle, not only sharing the physical burden of visiting her, but helping him put all the misery of that marriage – not behind him, exactly, but in some sort of context, so that he stops blaming himself and starts to see the whole dreadful business as something that can, if he looks at it properly, deepen and enrich his whole life. And not just his life but his work. He's a good writer, but once he's woven his past into his experience so that it's part of him, not just some dark, guilty room he's afraid to walk into, he'll be even better. I believe he can do it, and I do believe, very humbly, that I can support him, if only a little. . . .'

My voice shook. I saw, wonderingly, that in defending myself to Steve I had arrived, in some almost miraculous way, at the truth. What I had said was true as if an oracle had taken charge of my tongue and spoken through me. I had come to this meeting, I realised now, with very mixed motives. Among them a shameful one, a low, vulgar wish to show Steve that someone wanted me, even if he didn't. A silly girl, boasting to her ex-lover that she had landed a bigger fish out of the sea. Steve had known that, hit that nail on the head, hadn't he? He had hurt me, but he had done me a favour. I had always under-rated myself, been too humble to admit that there might be a finer side to my character. Steve had goaded me into being fair to myself and I felt grateful to him, and purified, and several years older, and very much happier. I had talked off the top of my head, out of anger with Steve, but I had spoken the truth, and it had matured and uplifted me. I felt very strange suddenly, but calm and still. No more doubts! I was finished with doubts as I was finished with Steve. Although I still loved him, he was part of my past now. I loved Eddie and knew, joyfully, that I was right to marry him: our marriage was right because I was bringing to it such a strong, beautiful purpose. Eddie wasn't perfect as I had once believed Steve to be but that was all to the good because perfection would have denied my best talents.

I said, 'I'm sorry if I was angry, dear Steve. But what I'm best at – if I'm good at anything – is supporting other people. Propping up their weaknesses, putting things right for them. Eddie's not really weak but he's vulnerable, and knowing that, knowing *all* his small faults, is just part of my loving him. And, since I'm not creative myself, it's a special bonus that he is. I can prop up his talent and see that he uses it. I can see why you're worried by the idea of Estelle. I expect I would be too, if I were in *your* place, looking at *me,* but the reality is nothing to worry about. She's a sad, sick woman, no threat at all.'

Priggish, prosy, sentimental young idiot! More than twenty years later, I think of that long-past Penelope with a certain benevolent tolerance (she was very young, after all) but also with some irritation. *Jealousy is so vile!* Ho, hum! Did St Penelope of Bleeding Hearts, Inc., really believe she was immune from that base emotion? Perhaps she did, at the time. But Eddie had written his famous novel for his first wife, for poor, damaged Estelle, and perhaps that had rankled. Did his second wife hope, at some point, in some part of her mind, that her talented husband would write one for her?

I don't know the answer. All I am sure of is that my idea – conceived while Eddie was writing his History of the Special Operations Executive, a mammoth task that occupied the first six years of our marriage – had not been, to begin with, a bad one. Since he'd shown Zed up as a traitor while writing of him as a hero, why not turn the tables? Another point of view – X's or Y's story, perhaps – that subtly exposed them as liars and reinstated their leader. A neat, technical trick that had inadvertently worked the first time – why not consciously use it a second? Eddie's research for the history had given him so much more background than he'd had before. Knowledge, and distance from his subject, would make a more solid book, a serious comment on the nature of treachery. *X. Y. and Zed* had really been a bit meretricious when one looked back at it. Eddie admitted this. He sometimes said he was amazed at his cheek in writing about something he knew so little about. Though one could know *too* much – there was always the danger that he might not be able to see the wood for the trees. I had argued with him, very patiently. One didn't have to use all one knew, but it must be an advantage to have it there, the bulk of the iceberg, hidden under the water. I remember the enthusiasm with which I produced this conventional analogy, one evening when Eddie was flushed with excitement and drink – and the pride I felt in the role I was playing. The young wife encouraging her genius husband! And he *had* been encouraged, had begun to make notes, drafted a chapter. Then he'd been asked (on the strength of the history) to write a series of television plays about the Resistance. He seemed eager to do this, and there seemed no great harm in it: a new form is always a challenge and it would give him a rest from his more 'serious' work. Unfortunately it turned out that he had a flair for neat plots and dialogue, as well as a physically timid man's fascination with danger and heroism, and so the success of the plays was counter-productive. When the first series ended and the producer suggested another, it was clear to me that Eddie was dissipating his energies. The dramatic form came too easily to him. It was seducing him from the hard grind of the novel. He said that the story had 'died on him', that he was tired, needed more time 'to get the whole thing into focus'. Lazy excuses, of course. I didn't blame him, or chide him, but my duty to try to safeguard his talent was clear.

And (I am sure of this now that I think about it) quite uncontaminated. If I flinched when Desdemona mentioned Estelle, it was only because I am so foolishly scared of this formidable woman. And because I have been used for too many years to searching my conscience, doubting my motives.

I say to Desdemona, 'I honestly don't think Estelle affects Eddie much any longer. And not just because she's far too batty to object to anything he might do. He's not even seen her for ages. Since she was moved to that bin up in Yorkshire he's only once been to visit.'

'Must be a relief for you, that,' Desdemona says.

'Oh, I never minded Estelle. The poor soul!'

'Well, you're very noble. I must say, in your place, I'd have minded. Looking up at that dotty tower every time I went shopping and thinking, There's the first Mrs Eddie locked away there! Like a Thurber cartoon. But I wasn't thinking she might make any trouble – as you say, she's quite batty – just that as long as she's alive Eddie might feel some sort of commitment to putting the record straight. You know what a funny, honourable old fellow he is!'

The amused affection with which she speaks about Eddie has a strange effect on me. I feel hurt and jealous. This is silly, of course. I am *glad* Desdemona is so fond of Eddie and so ready to help him. On the other hand, the warmth in her voice is a bit pointed, surely? As if she means to make it quite clear to me that she is on Eddie's side in this matter, not mine.

I say, quickly, 'Oh, I do know that, Des. He's a good man – pure gold! If he wasn't, it might not be so hard to leave him.'

Desdemona does not answer this. It is not, perhaps, worth an answer. She says, 'If Estelle were dead, he might feel free to do something quite different.'

'Do you think that he should?'

'Lord – I don't know. I wouldn't presume to advise him. I think his telly stuff is really quite excellent. Perhaps he should stick to it.'

'But, Des, he's a *novelist.*'

'He wrote one novel, dear. Still in print, which is fairly remarkable after so long, and of course we'd be delighted to think there might be another from him sometime. All I mean is, as his publishers, we're not depending on it for our bread and butter.'

'Neither is he. Sometimes I think that's his trouble. If he really had to work for his living.'

I reflect, uncomfortably, that I do not work for mine. At least, this is how Desdemona might see it. From her point of view I am a stay-at-home hausfrau, a kept woman whose work on the Bench, being unpaid, can be put down as a nice little hobby. What right have I to complain about my man's idleness when I have never brought home any bacon! Working women like Desdemona see domestic labour as a cosy retreat. Well, perhaps it is. I have never been inclined to join that particular battle let alone march in the Women's Lib. ranks. Not because I like the idea of being a chattel, a second-class citizen, but because it has always seemed to me that in most walks of life the men have the worst of it. Compared with a shift down a coal-mine, washing dishes is a soft option, and a businessman's ulcers are a good deal more painful than a captive wife's boredom. But of course I have never seen myself as a captive wife. I have been Eddie's research assistant, his secretary, his Muse, the nurse to his talents. . . .

I say, 'Oh, that sounds ghastly. I must sound to you like a selfish, middle-class wife flogging her husband into his coronary. But you know it's not like that. Eddie could sit on his backside till Doomsday and I wouldn't complain if I didn't believe his work was important. If you don't think it is, I suppose it must seem to you that I have simply been wasting my time, but I just don't agree with you. I think Eddie will write something really very special one day. I may not have helped him as much as I hoped to – perhaps going off now may be one of the best things I have done for him! – but I have always believed in him *totally*. I may have been a slave-driver, but in a good cause. Or it seemed a good cause to me.'

My throat is suddenly aching and burning with imminent tears. Oh, the shame and waste of it all! Eddie's talent wasted, my devotion; all frail, human hopes. I could weep but cannot bear Desdemona to hear me. I swallow hard, make myself breathe deeply and steadily, force a stiff smile to my lips although no one can see.

Desdemona says, 'You don't have to defend yourself to me, dear.'

Part Three

It is hard to defend oneself eloquently. Those who do are not always the educated, the highly articulate. A middle-aged labourer, charged with refusing to send his son to school, comes to court clutching a letter from his wife. She has written down what he wants to say; will the Bench read it? He can't speak for himself, the words will 'choke up in his throat'. Persuaded to try, he stumbles and sweats, and then, suddenly, passion seizes his tongue. . . .

'Here I stand now. I can't read nor write. I've never told no one before only my wife; but I'm telling you now that the shame has humbled me all my life long. I wanted a better chance for my boy, but he's thirteen years of age and he sits at the back of the class and they don't teach him nothing. It's a fine school to look at, all glass and big playing-fields, but it's all play they do there, the ones in the D stream. What they call projects. One term they was sent out to paint old people's houses, and the last term he was there he was made to exercise dogs from the kennels. I never said nothing about the house-painting – it's right they should teach them to help the old people – but when he came home and said he'd been out with the dogs, that stuck in my gullet. That's all, I said. Finish! I rang the Headmaster but he said, "Write a letter." I can't write, so I kept the boy home to show what I felt. My boy's slow, but he'd learn if they tried to teach him; that's what he's supposed to go to school for, isn't it? Education is books not walking dogs for rich people. It's a wicked shame and a waste, to my mind. The law says I must send my son to this school. Why doesn't the law see that they teach him, not waste him the way that they're doing, keeping him down so he'll be fit for nothing time they have finished but emptying dustbins.' His eyes flash burning scorn at the Bench as he waves his wife's letter and tears it to pieces in front of them. 'That's all she set down for me here, in this piece of paper. All I wanted to say. To ask how you'd feel, all you good people, if it was one of your children being used like my boy, thrown on the tip like some old piece of garbage.'

Few manage to put their point of view so effectively. Most people prefer their actions to be defended by others. By some kind, powerful friend. Everyone has dreams about this, perhaps? *Penelope is too humble to put her own case, but I am telling you now – and my word is law – that she is basically a very good person, almost a saint, a heroine on life's battlefield.*

Is this what I want? No, of course not. Only the truth, revealed to the awed and listening multitude by some unimpeachable source, trumpeted from battlements, delivered on tablets from some divine mountain-top. The few small stains on my character, my minor tumbles from grace, can be freely admitted because it is sinful to wish to be perfect. *Penelope has tried to be good* is the best accolade.

Back in court for the afternoon session, the Judge wigged and robed on my left, Goggle Eyes on his other side, I wince as I think how Desdemona would laugh at this fantasy. Never apologise, never explain, is the robust rule she has always lived by. Perhaps her sexual tastes have contributed to this truculent attitude but, whatever the cause, the effect is intimidating. You cannot stand up for yourself in her presence; it feels too much like weakness. All the same, I wish I had tried. It would have been more dignified to produce a small spurt of anger – for Eddie's sake, if not for my own. I was taken aback; that was the trouble. I had been so sure Desdemona valued Eddie's work as much as I did; had relied on her, really, to carry the torch for him once I had gone. I should have said so, quite plainly. No anger was necessary, just a calm statement of what I considered a good publisher's duty to be. Instead, I had thanked her for offering to go and get drunk with my husband – and taken my frustration out on my lover....

I was so curt when I telephoned. No endearments – just the time of the train I was catching. As if I were making a business appointment. And when he sounded surprised it made me resentful. I was leaving Eddie for him. What more did he want? Or was I resentful because Desdemona had made me feel guilty? Oh, it defeated logic. The emotion I had felt at that moment, a sudden access of hot, spiteful rage, is too confused to be analysed. There is no point in trying; it is too unimportant. He won't blame me because I was sharp when he asked why I couldn't catch an earlier train. We have the rest of our lives to be happy in, an extra hour or so now hardly matters. But I didn't say that. Nor told him why I would have to be late. I said, 'Oh, for God's sake, if it's too inconvenient, don't bother to come to the station; I'll get a taxi.' And slammed the telephone down before he could answer.

I feel dreadful now; sick with shame and anxiety. But there is nothing I can do. Not for several hours, anyway. I am stuck here, in the Crown Court, and counsel has just called the defendant into the witness-box. Abel Binder, holding the Testament in his right hand and swearing to tell the truth, the whole truth. A large promise that he seems to take seriously: his rosy face has lost colour and his square, red hand trembles as he puts the book down and faces his counsel. How does he feel? Nervous, obviously; stomach churning, sweat glands working overtime. But there must also be a certain not wholly unpleasant excitement. If he has not fallen foul of the law before, this is the first time so much of society's money and time will have been spent on him in one day. Everyone in the court except the lay magistrates (and of course the defendant) is paid to be here – Judge, ushers, clerks, lawyers, jury – and there is also the huge cost of maintaining this building, lighting on dark days, heating in winter, cleaning it, equipping it with crockery in the dining-room, disposable towels in the toilets, planting out bulbs in the flower-beds. If he had been tried summarily, in my local court, we could probably have dealt with his case in about thirty minutes, but he has chosen to protest his innocence here, in front of a judge and a jury. It is unlikely that he thinks of the cost to the nation this choice had entailed but he must be aware that the whole stately, cumbersome ritual has been staged for his benefit. If he has any feeling for theatre he may even be looking forward by now to putting on a performance. Perhaps, as the morning dragged on and he watched the prosecution witnesses giving their evidence, he began to welcome the prospect of taking his turn in the box. His chance to declare himself.

His counsel is an elderly man with a pointed head and narrow, sloping shoulders that make him look bottom-heavy, like a penguin. He has a long, thin, red nose and a nasal, slightly whining delivery. Abel answers his preliminary questions in a clear, polite voice. He agrees that he is married and works as a tractor-driver. This is his only skill. He left school at fifteen, took no examinations, served no apprenticeship; all he knows about motor cars is what he has taught himself. He and his wife live with her parents. They are on the list for a council flat but have not yet acquired enough 'points' to be offered one. The old people's house is small, with no bathroom and only an outside toilet. Abel and his wife have a bedroom, and their daughter sleeps with them; their baby son in a cot on the landing. He gets on with his parents-in-law, but crowded conditions sometimes make difficulties. When the baby cries at night he wakes up the household, and there is nowhere to sit in the evening except round the telly. This is one of the reasons he spends so much time up at the garages. 'A bit of peace and quiet there,' he volunteers, smiling pleasantly.

Counsel nods and smiles back. He rocks on his heels, shrugging his shabby gown up on his shoulders, and pauses to glance at the jury. He is pleased with the impression his client is making, presenting himself as a decent young fellow, not overburdened with brains, perhaps, but uncomplaining and easy-going and willing. Although society has not given him much, neither an inside lavatory nor much education – he was, almost certainly, one of those boys at the back of the class – he has no chip on his shoulder, is not one of those grouchy layabouts who whine that the world owes them a fat living. From a middle-class point of view, in fact, an ideal working-class man; deferential, hard-working, content with his place on the bottom rung of the ladder, driving his tractor, mending richer men's motor cars, sleeping with his wife in a small, crowded, old house with thin walls that doesn't belong to him.

Counsel says, 'Well, we all know it's not easy, living with parents when one is married,' and watching Abel, seeing his sudden grin, I think of the tell-tale clanging of bedsprings.

I wasn't shocked by Eddie's antics when we got married. If this shy man needed a bit of a romp to get himself going, chasing me round the room with wild yells, pretending to be a Red Indian, or pouncing on me, growling through his teeth like a lion or bear, what did it matter? I was young and adaptable; I knew Eddie had sexual fears and had braced myself to be tolerant. But the noise he made was inhibiting. On our honeymoon in the Italian hotel, once I had heard the man next door cough and turn up the radio, I was too embarrassed to play Eddie's games any longer.

'I'm sorry,' he said, crouching naked and limp on the bed, belly sweating, eyes weakly tear-filled. 'My sweetie, my blossom. Please try to forgive me.'

'There's nothing to forgive, darling. I love you.' I was sure this was true. His anguished humility was exciting; the sight of this large, powerful man humble and helpless before me made me feel strong and protective. I would look after him, comfort and cure him. I said soothingly, 'It's my fault really. I'm being silly. There's absolutely no reason why we shouldn't have fun any way that we want to. But it puts me off, knowing people can hear. It'll be all right once we get home. Please don't cry, Eddie.'

If we had had to share a house with our parents, or rent a small flat with listening neighbours, we would have had to live like brother and sister. Luckily, Eddie's house in Cedar Grove, the house he had bought so that he could be near Estelle in the hospital, was solid and private. And perhaps (so I thought to begin with) if I were kind and loving and patient he might grow in confidence, be able to manage without these peculiar rituals.

The trouble was, they seemed so ludicrous to me. If he had been sadistic, hurt me or beaten me, I could have seen him as a dark, troubled hero. As it was, his childish pretences only inspired me to giggle. Although I never let him know this, moaning beneath him with fake cries of pleasure, I began to resent being made to put on a performance. I couldn't admit my resentment of course – that would have meant admitting to failure – but told myself, humorously, that I really preferred him with his clothes on. Without them he made such a fool of himself, slavering over me like a big, clumsy dog, idiotically smiling. There were two Eddies, it seemed : the kind, decent, clothed man whom I loved and admired for his dignity and gentle intelligence, and whose genius I meant to nurture; and the fat, naked, ridiculous, slobbering fool whose folly I had to suffer. I did suffer it, out of duty and pity, only rarely resorting to the excuse of headaches or tiredness, but was glad when his aunts came to stay, sweet, twittering, unmarried ladies whose virginal ears must not be offended. Aunt Emma and Aunt Joan were his mother's sisters; Aunt Philomena his father's. They were devoted to Eddie and accustomed to making protracted visits to keep house for him. 'We've kept in close touch since his dear mother died,' Aunt Emma said. 'Not to take her place, naturally – that wouldn't be possible – but they were so fond of each other we knew there would be a dreadful gap once she'd gone. And, when poor Estelle first got ill and he was so miserable, we drew up a kind of rota between us. He was always such a sensitive boy, we didn't want him to be left alone, brooding. Of course now he's happily married it's different. Young couples like to be on their own. I think his other aunties may not quite realise that, but you can tell *me*, dear Penelope, if you'd rather not have us. I shan't be offended and I can drop a sly hint or two where it's needed.'

'But I love you to come,' I cried eagerly. 'It's lovely for me to have some relations! I've so few of my own.'

And to Eddie, 'They're old and they love you. It would be nicer to be by ourselves a bit more, I know that, but I don't want them to feel shut out. I mean, they don't come *so* often, do they? And they've been so sweet to me, made me feel they really do like and welcome me.'

'Why shouldn't they?'

'Because I'm a poor girl who's nabbed their rich nephew. They might think I was after your money.'

His eyes widened with amazement and laugher. 'My pettikins, my *funny* one! If they think anything, they think I'm astonishingly lucky. You're too good for me, don't you know that? I don't think you do. I don't think you know how good and unselfish you are. Why shouldn't they be sweet to you? You're so sweet to them. My funny old aunts.' He blinked and blushed patchily. 'Sweet to me, too. My own blessing!'

Did *he* bless his aunts' presence too, and for the same reason I did? I wondered sometimes, watching him play chess with Aunt Emma – the 'brainy' one – or hold skeins of wool for Aunt Joan, who knitted him endless, thick, indestructible sweaters. Perhaps he was secretly scared of the sexual challenge that faced him when we were alone. Or perhaps, more simply, he didn't find me attractive. It was perverse, in the circumstances, to let this upset me, but sometimes I went to bed early, leaving him drinking whisky and watching television with one old aunt or another, and wept

under the blankets. I would never know – Eddie was too kind a
man to tell the truth about something like that. He had told me
he was impotent with Estelle, but perhaps he had lied and, in his
heart, compared me unfavourably. Estelle was a hideous, mad,
middle-aged woman, and it was shameful to be jealous of her.
Degrading even to think of her in bed with Eddie! But she had
been pretty once. There was a photograph of her in Eddie's study;
dark-lipped and small-featured with soft, fluffy hair. Eddie had
said, 'Do you mind, pet? I'll put it away if you do. I haven't done
it before because it seemed a bit silly. A bit deliberate. After all,
you'd been in my study before we were married and seen it was
there.'

'Of course I don't mind. It's stupid to mind.'

'Which do you mean, honey drop?'

'Both. It's stupid to mind, and I *don't* mind.'

'Sure?'

'Quite sure.' I was mildly irritated. *His* study, after all, *his* first
wife. Why not his decision. 'Why should I make up your mind
for you? Are you so lazy?'

'Fairly, my dove. Sentimental and superstitious is what I'm being
just now, though. I don't much like Estelle's picture there, actually.
And, if you really minded, I'd be happy to shove it away in a
drawer. But I feel a bit *funny* doing it off my own bat!' He
rubbed at his eyes with his knuckles and when he took his hands
away I saw his tears shining. He smiled at me tremulously. 'I did
love her once and now she's locked away, a quite different person,
quite horribly changed, and it seems wicked to want to forget
what she used to be like. Do you see, angel? Taking her picture
down is a bit like making an end of her altogether.'

'I can't see that whatever you do with her photograph now can
make the slightest difference to her one way or another.'

'No. No, of course not.' His pink face was troubled and sly.
He grabbed at me, imprisoning my hands between his damp
palms. 'Oh, my dear one, my baby, you are *good* for me. So crisp

and cool and so sensible. I have such nightmares, still, about her! I'm so muddled and stupid. You'll have to take me in hand. Do you mind?'

I was touched. He needed me and I loved him for it. At the same time his sweating hands, holding me so hotly and tightly, made me uncomfortable. I loved him but shuddered away from him physically. This seemed dreadful! It *was* dreadful! He would be so humiliated and hurt if he knew, and that was the last thing I wanted. It seemed so unfair! I wanted to be a good wife, meant to concentrate all my strong, loving energy on it, but my body refused to co-operate. A foolish, mechanical failure! I had read somewhere about a man who was impotent with his wife until he fractured his spine in a road accident. After that he was able to make love to his wife because the fears that beset him could no longer send anxious messages from his brain through the spinal-cord path to his penis. That was all sex was for a man – a straight reflex action. Since I was a woman my spinal cord did not need to be severed. I only had to dissemble. Internal laughter bubbled up like a sweet, cleansing spring; I laughed aloud and withdrew my hand gently. 'Darling, of course I don't mind. You old silly. My dear old, silly old teddy bear! It's why I married you, isn't it? To look after you.'

Why had I married him, *really*? Would I have mentioned his money, out of the blue like that, if it had not been a factor? Oh, of course I had been impressed by the climate of his life, his expensive car, his successful book, his Eton education, his rich relations. I was a poor, young, snobbish girl, grateful for the social and financial security he was offering me. But I did love him too; was sorry for him because he had a mad wife, wanted to comfort and help him. Would this impulse have been any purer if he had been a dustman? Or a tractor-driver, like Abel Binder? Not necessarily. Some women are sexually aroused by men they can see as inferior. But it is crazy to argue this way. Motives are hard to get at; even harder to be honest about. And it is not always honest to be hard on oneself. The shabbiest reasons are not always the 'real' ones, just because we have to dig in the mud for them. Truth can often be seen floating crystal clear on the surface; sometimes people do mean what they say, and say what they mean.

There is no reason to doubt Abel Binder's wholesome simplicity. He likes mending cars and was happy to advise the student about his old wreck. 'Though it was only talk really, he wasn't too keen to get his hands dirty,' Abel says, smiling his pleasant smile. He doesn't resent this lordly attitude; seems, indeed, to have enjoyed the young student's company. They had gone to the pub one or two evenings, had a few beers together. Abel didn't know he was at university. It didn't occur to him, when the student stopped turning up at the garages, that he might have gone back to college. He assumed he'd simply lost interest in stripping down his old car. 'A big job, once he'd started. I thought he didn't feel up to it. Like it was a bit of game to him.'

'That's what you thought at the time? That he'd abandoned the car?'

'Well, not at once. I didn't really think nothing at first. Only when the couple came and said they'd been to the Council and rented that same garage the Mercedes was in. I wasn't to know there'd been a mix-up and they'd got the wrong one. I just said to myself, Well, he's not paid his rent, so he's dumped it.'

'Yes. I see. And, when the scrap-dealer offered to take the Mercedes away, what were your feelings then?'

'I was a bit fed up, getting him down to the yard for nothing. My stuff had been nicked, what he'd come for. I thought he might just as well have the old car for his trouble. It wasn't no use, just in the way there, now these people wanted the garage to put their car in.'

'You were doing them a good turn?'

'Sort of, I suppose. I didn't think much about it.'

Honest Abel! Clearly his motives were only mildly benevolent, but if he picked up a fiver helping the dealer remove the old wreck was that very venal? He isn't a villain but an honest young man trapped by a combination of small, foolish circumstances and, the emotional state I am in, he has begun to look to me like a hero. When the prosecuting counsel gets up to examine him, a fierce dislike seizes me. This lawyer has pitted skin, yellow teeth, and the tone of his voice is unpleasantly sneering. Apparently he finds Abel's protestations of innocence quite incredible. He'd had some of his own stuff pinched from the yard, hadn't he? Old tyres, bumper bars – worth a bit as scrap, weren't they? But instead of ringing the police as a good citizen would normally do – as the student had done, indeed, as soon as he found his car gone – he had simply sold something that wasn't his property. A sort of tit-for-tat operation? And, perhaps, a small element of resentment? Abel was a hard-working man, supporting a family. He couldn't afford a car. There was this idle fellow, this student, who'd taken up Abel's time, picked his brains. What right had he to two cars when Abel had none?

Abel says equably, 'There's plenty of people better off than me. I don't bother about it.'

'I suggest that, when the opportunity came, you were quite ready to take it. That selling this young man's car was a way of getting a bit of your own back?'

'No, sir.'

Counsel scratches the side of his nose with his index finger and looks at his papers as if there may be something there he has forgotten to mention. But he is only pausing for dramatic effect. I hate him for this weary device. I think: *You bloody cheap trickster,* as he says, grinning evilly, 'Why did you lie to him, then, when he came? If you thought you'd done nothing wrong, selling his car, why did you tell him you didn't know what had happened to it?'

'I thought he'd make trouble.'

'Really? Why should you think that?'

'He was that sort.'

'I see.' Counsel pauses again, sucks at his yellow teeth. 'Can you explain to me what you mean by that statement?'

Abel looks at him in defeated silence. I long to speak up for him, answer this sneering monster. The student is an arrogant, spoiled, middle-class puppy brought up to believe the chief purpose of law is to safeguard his wretched possessions. Society is constructed to safeguard his interests, not Abel's, and Abel knows it. He doesn't know how to say this, nor would it help him much if he did. He mutters at last, 'I don't know.'

Counsel sighs. 'You hoped he'd just go away and forget all about it?'

Abel says, goaded, 'I didn't *hope* nothing. I just saw it looked bad and I didn't know what to do. I'd have given him the five pounds if I'd thought he'd have taken it.' He hesitates, ill at ease suddenly – should he have said this? His case seems so simple but the tricky acrobatics of legal procedure have sown doubts in his mind, laid explosive traps all around him. He feels like a man in a minefield, afraid to take a step one way or another. But time is running out. He looks up at the Judge and speaks to him directly and desperately, hoping against hope that this superior wigged and robed being can be trusted to rescue him. 'As soon as he turned up that day I knew I'd done wrong. But I didn't know it till then, sir. On my oath. I thought it was all right what I'd done with the car, when I did it. But then, when he came, I just reckoned he wouldn't believe me.'

I look at the jury and wonder if they will. Their faces are stiff, perhaps hiding boredom. They appear to be listening (at least, at this moment, no one is yawning or scratching or shuffling cramped buttocks), but they look to me less like real people with sorrows and hopes, jobs and families, than waxworks in a Museum of Human Types: the Intelligent Lady, the Young Tart, the Ape Man, the Honest Labourer. I do not wonder about them as I wonder about Abel Binder. Like the clerks and the ushers, the lawyers and magistrates, they are part of the furniture of the court. Stage props, not actors.

It is always the defendants who interest me in these legal theatricals. I know so much about them, of course; have read social reports, antecedents, heard the laconic testimony of police officers, the partisan pleading of lawyers. Or perhaps I feel guilty because I have judged them and that makes me remember them. Whatever the reason, the fact is that they live on in my imagination, complaining, justifying, weeping, apologising, lying, reeling off platitudes, long after they have appeared before me. My mind is a snapshot album composed of their faces. I turn the pages and they stare up at me, frail and defeated, agitated, aggressive, defiant or fearful – all so instantly recognisable that it amazes me, sometimes, that ears, noses and mouths can be arranged in so many different ways, that nature can take such infinite trouble, be so endlessly inventive with such little people. For my rogues' picture gallery contains few important criminals. My clients do not commit murder or genocide or arson or treason or piracy on the high seas. They steal lengths of lead piping. They cheat the railways by travelling with out-of-date tickets or no tickets at all. They neglect their children; loiter with intent; cause minor affrays outside public houses; insult the police; break windows; assault each other causing bodily harm. They carry offensive weapons : walking-sticks or bicycle-chains or flick-knives. They go equipped for stealing, sometimes in imaginative ways. Two empty soup-tins, each with one end removed, a wad of cotton wool and a small bottle half-full of water make an excellent hiding-place for jewels between the cotton packaging and the bottle. The two tins are fitted together giving the appearance of one, and placed in a basket of innocent groceries. If picked up and shaken by some suspicious police officer, the liquid in the small bottle will sound exactly like soup in a tin.

Sad, perhaps, that such larky ingenuity should have to be

punished. Impossible not to reflect that if the inventor of this clever contraption had been luckier in his origins, in his background and education, his talents might have been put to some more socially acceptable use. He might, for example, have split the atom and ended up with a knighthood instead of in prison. Better, in some ways, if he had stuck to his soup-tins, but we are perversely selective in our perception of criminal behaviour. It is not entirely frivolous to argue that one of the causes of crime is the laws we make to prevent it.

As Adam argued last autumn. Found guilty of possessing and supplying cannabis resin, fined two hundred pounds and given a suspended sentence, he was indignant, not penitent. Quoting John Stuart Mill at me, only in his own, rather less elegant, words. 'It's so bloody stupid, Aunt Pen. I mean, if there's any harm in the stuff, which I don't think there is personally, it only harms me and the one or two friends I passed it on to, just as a favour. And what fucking business is that of anyone else's? I mean, I'm not actually drawn to that particular scene, but it's so fucking illogical that it's enough to make one want to get into it in a really big way. Drug-running with the big boys. I mean, as a *protest*. I mean. . . .'

I said, 'Please stop saying "I mean". You're quite fluent enough to express yourself without repetition of that lazy kind.'

'All right, dear. Sorry if my misuse of language offends your sensitive ears. What I was going to say was, look at the Boston Tea Party,' Adam said, smiling sweetly. We were lunching together, celebrating the fact that he had not been sent to prison. This had seemed to me a real possibility, and I was astonished that Adam had faced it so calmly. Was he insensitive, perhaps, like his mother? Although April had known the date Adam's case was set down to be heard, she had left, two weeks earlier, for a holiday in the Bahamas. I had gone to court with him and paid his fine –

which would have been smaller, I guessed, if he had cut his hair before appearing in front of the magistrates. I thought his dark, shining mane suited him, curling thickly round his pale, beautiful face and over his denim-clad shoulders, but knew that the balding, middle-aged men on the Bench were unlikely to share my opinion. ('A red rag to ageing bulls,' I told Adam, speaking lightly, hoping to coax him, but he had just laughed and said, 'Oh, Aunt Pen, I do love you, but I can't cut it, even for you; it's the *principle*.')

He said now, 'The Americans thought the King of England had no right to tax their tea, so they emptied it into Boston harbour. I happen to think *personally* that they were behaving quite properly. No one has a duty to obey an unjust law, do they? Though I suppose *you* won't agree with me.' He laughed with fine, theatrical scorn. 'You're part of the Law and Order Establishment. Them against Us!'

I thought: I ought to get angry. But I was too happy. So glad he was free, sitting with me in this comfortable restaurant instead of kicking his heels in the cells waiting for the van to take him to prison. He must have been frightened of that, in his heart. He had hidden his fear from me, to keep *my* spirits up! We had waited for over two hours for his name to be called, on a hard bench in the chilly corridor outside the court, and he had been cheerful and considerate the whole time, chatting away to the other defendants as if this was a social occasion, and apologising to me for the trouble he'd put me to. 'All the same, this is a *good* experience for you, Auntie Pen! Now you know how the other half live. At least you know one thing you may not have known about them before. The reason why the criminal classes are lethargic and always have colds is because they spend most of their time in draughty corridors waiting for something to happen.'

Of course he wasn't insensitive. He was gay (in the good, old-fashioned sense of that abused word) and courageous.

I said, smiling at him across the table, 'I do agree with you, as it happens, about the Boston Tea Party. Although in that case they weren't protesting against an unjust law, but against the legitimacy of the law-making authority. Not quite the same thing as smoking pot because you happen to think there's no harm in it.'

'I don't see much difference. All I'm trying to say is that crime is what the law says is crime. By *definition*, Aunt Pen. And, since laws are made by a tiny minority and enforced on the rest of us, they're bound to be in the interests of that minority, aren't they? Which is why you get such a shocking bias in the interests of property. A few rich men passing laws so that they can hang on to their ill-gotten gains. If you bash someone up you get a much lighter sentence than if you pinch something. I think that's fucking disgusting.'

I said helplessly, fondly, '*Dear* Adam! Of course it's true that, if there wasn't a law against burglary, breaking into someone's house wouldn't be, according to that kind of medieval logic, a crime. And of course some fringe laws are silly. I mean. . . .'

He laughed with delight, shaking his clean, curling locks, laughing eyes plum-dark and gleaming. 'Pen! Auntie Pen, *darling*!'

'Shut up, Adam. I was going to say that perhaps a law saying people mustn't bathe naked is stupid because bathing naked harms no one. But serious crimes – theft and murder and so on – have always been crime, in any civilised society. Most uncivilised ones too, for that matter. And is the definition of crime, as you've given it, really so very foolish? If you lived in a Greek city state, say, you wouldn't think so. You'd accept that the laws you lived by were the laws that were made by that state. By definition. Without question!'

He was watching me with a mocking expression. He shook his head slowly. 'It doesn't suit you, dear. Really it doesn't. Not your thing at all. I don't know how you ever thought it could be. How you got into it. How you ever became a magistrate in the first place!'

'You know perfectly well, idiot boy. My name was put forward to the Lord Chancellor's selection committee by the local Labour party.'

'I don't mean that. I meant *why*! You didn't have to take it on, did you?'

'No. But I was asked, and it seemed a worthwhile thing to do. I like to be useful.'

'You like power, you mean.' Adam wrinkled his nose as if he smelled something bad. 'Isn't that rather disgusting?'

'If it was the only reason, it would be. But I hope it isn't.'

'It'll change you in the end. Whatever you *hope*, it'll change you. You'll find you'll be corrupted, unable to make real moral judgements. Oh, I don't see any signs yet. I mean, you're a bit harder in some ways than you used to be, but you're still basically *normal*.'

'Thank you, dear Adam.'

He regarded me primly. 'I'm serious, dear.'

'So am I.' I laughed at him, joyful suddenly: I was a little drunk and arguing with Adam was exhilarating, like a drunken party flirtation. 'It's normal to enjoy having a hand in running things. More normal, I'd think, than opting out and grumbling because things are done badly. Of course I like feeling important but I don't think I'm corrupted by it. In fact, quite the opposite. I never expected much, or thought much of myself, and it's done me good these last eight years or so to feel – well – a person of consequence.'

I pulled a wry face to show I knew this was comic.

'A sense of identity,' Adam said. 'What a ghastly awful platitude. Really, Aunt Pen.'

I smiled, but his sneering tone hurt me. I had tried to be honest and it seemed I had just sounded naïve and stupid to him.

I said, 'It was you said it, not me. I never mentioned a sense of identity. All I admitted to was feeling a bit stronger and a bit more sure of myself because other people obviously thought I was competent to do this particular thing. And I thought if I said one ought to do one's bit to help others, play a part in society, you'd call it a load of old crap, or some such charming expression.'

'It's a funny way to help people, I must say. Fining them and sending them off to the nick.' Adam sighed deeply, and then, looking up from the coffee cup he was fiddling with, grinned at me wickedly. 'Not that I ought to mind that if I'm strictly logical. I really hate all this fucking cant about helping others that people go in for. It's so fucking *false*. My generation is worse than yours, actually. They want to be nurses or social workers and look after what they will call the Handicapped. I think it's sick. Though one knows why they want to do it. They don't know how to run their own lives so they compensate by messing up other people's. Most bossy people are inadequate, really.'

I said, 'Thank you, dear Adam.'

Steve had said, 'Of course you must be a magistrate, darling. People like you are needed on the Bench. All those stuffed shirts! You'd be a breath of fresh air.'

He had laughed, amazed that I should hesitate for a moment, or question his views of the kind of magistrate I should be. His own life was dedicated to rescue work. He worked for a firm of criminal solicitors, taking on legal-aid cases in the lower courts seeing his clients as victims, not villains, his own role as knightly. He rode to court on a second-hand Honda (he considered a car an unnecessary luxury), fair hair curling beneath his crash-helmet. When his clients went to prison he visited them and kept in touch with their families. One evening a week he spent helping his local member of Parliament at the 'surgery' she ran for her constituents in the front room of the suburban house where she lived with her widowed mother. The M.P. was in her thirties but she dressed like a little girl in short tweed skirts, matching sweaters, and long, white socks. In the House (Steve told me proudly) she was known as Lolita.

Steve called her Lolly. He admired her tremendously; this was clear from the shining way his eyes watched her as she talked or moved round the room. She wasn't pretty, with a high, pale, slightly greasy forehead and thinning dark hair, but her soft unpainted mouth and large, liquid eyes made her touching, and her frail childish body was definitely sexy.

Or so Eddie said, when Steve brought her to dine with us.

'Definitely sexy, Pen, duckie. Not everyone's cup of tea, not mine in fact, but a lot of men would find her attractive. It's that abandoned-waif look. Sad, a bit grubby, mind on higher things, but a *mind*. That's always worth having.'

'Do you think Steve goes to bed with her?' I spoke without thinking, and Eddie looked at me oddly.

'Couldn't say, lovey-dove. I think he might marry her. She's the first girl he's ever introduced to us, isn't she? But, as to the other, I'm the last chap to ask about that sort of thing.'

I couldn't ask Steve. We were not on those sort of terms any longer. Since my marriage, we had seen each other so rarely. Although we had kept in touch, sending comic birthday-cards, small presents at Christmas, we had only met three or four times a year and then usually at weekends when Eve came to stay and we asked him to Sunday lunch with his mother. I had watched him grow leaner and older, but the essential change in him, from a rather conventional young man to a distinctly eccentric middle-aged one, had happened so gradually I had barely noticed it. Or perhaps he had always been a kind of Don Quixote, the romantic crusader always there in the bud, so to speak, so that when it unfolded the flowering was perfectly natural – not a change, but a development. Certainly, that night I went to his flat, after the first panicky moment when he opened the door and seemed like a stranger, the next he was Steve again as I had always known him; dear Steve, whom I loved.

Eddie was in America. I had been asked if I would consider becoming a magistrate. I was flattered and nervous. I wanted to talk to someone, and Steve seemed the obvious person. It was an excuse, though I didn't realise that to begin with. All I knew was that when I had telephoned Steve, after I put the receiver down, I was trembling. My hands shook, my pulse raced – I felt sick with excitement like a girl who has just made her first assignation. It was stupid, of course. I knew it was stupid. I told myself so. I wasn't a girl, I was a woman in her thirty-ninth year, a good wife and mother whose growing daughters were doing their homework downstairs in the kitchen. And although Steve had once, long ago, been my lover he was someone I barely knew now: a middle-aged, slightly eccentric solicitor who was going to marry a Member of Parliament. This was a few weeks after he brought Lolly to dinner and Eddie had said he might marry her.

I told the girls I was going to see Uncle Steve. I said they must finish their homework before they watched television and that they must be in bed by ten-thirty. They looked up from their books, bright-eyed, shining-faced, nodding solemnly. Louise had braces on her teeth; Jenny a bruised cheek from a wildly aimed hockey-stick. When I kissed them, they both smelled of childhood.

The suburb where Steve lived was on our side of London. I drove there slowly and carefully. If I were going to be a magistrate I would have to be careful not to break the speed limit. Eddie would have to be more careful too. He was such an erratic driver, creeping timidly along on wide, open roads and then, suddenly, in busy towns, veering across traffic-lanes like a lunatic, screeching round corners and through red lights, horn wildly blaring. Driving to visit Steve I thought about Eddie and wondered why he was such a menace. Was he acting out some dark fantasy about death and destruction when he got behind the wheel of a car? As he acted it out in his sex life. I had said to him, a few months ago, after a particularly boisterous episode, 'One day you'll come charging after me with that axe and the head will fly off and kill me.' I had only been joking, but the effect on him had been shattering. He had turned pale as death and collapsed on the bed, shaking and shuddering. I couldn't comfort him; when I put my arms round him he pushed me away and buried his face in the pillow. I had tried to talk to him later, when he was calmer, but he refused to discuss what had happened.

I thought: I wish I could tell someone about this. My marriage is such a failure that my husband wishes me dead. Should I tell Steve? I laughed, and the steering-wheel shook in my hands. Steve would think I was mad. One of those dreadful mad women who make obscene confessions about their sex lives at parties. No. No, of course he wouldn't think that. He would take it seriously. I thought: How do I know how he'd take it? I know nothing about him.

Steve's flat was on the top floor of a converted old house. There were several dustbins outside and a collection of empty, unwashed milk-bottles. The front door was open and I walked up four flights and knocked on Steve's door. He opened it immediately – as if he had been waiting behind it. He said, 'Oh, there you are! I've made some coffee.'

I sat down in a leather armchair in which the springs sagged so deeply my behind touched the floor. Steve gave me coffee in a blue-and-white mug. He said, 'Would you like a sandwich?' and looked round rather vaguely as if he hoped to spy one, lurking among the toppling piles of books on the floor or on the cluttered desk. I thought he had probably not eaten this evening. I said, 'Yes, if it's not too much trouble,' and watched through the open door that led to the kitchen while he took slices of bread from a crumpled packet and hacked at a lump of cheese. The kitchen was narrow and untidy and dirty, the table and sink unit were covered with unwashed dishes and pans; there was a distinct smell of rancid fat and blocked drains. I called out, 'Do you want help,' and he said, 'No,' rather sharply. He came back into the room and gave me the sandwich.

I said, 'Aren't you having one?'

'No. I eat at lunch-time. In a pub, usually.'

'Not at night? I mean, it looks as if you cook sometimes.'

'Oh, I open tins. When people drop by.' He folded himself into a chair as old and springless as the one I sat in. His knees rose to his chin and he regarded me warily over them.

I bit into the sandwich. The bread was stale and tasted of mildew. 'What sort of people?'

He grinned. 'Villains, mostly. Members of Parliament. Prospective lady magistrates. Leave that sandwich if it's really too nasty. If I'd known you were coming I'd have baked a cake. Got some drink, anyway. Do you want a drink? I'm not sure, but I think there might be some whisky.'

He was so nervous I began to feel easier. 'Does Lolly come here?'

'Sometimes. Do you mean, how can she bear it? Or why doesn't she clean the place up a bit?'

'Neither,' I lied. 'You could get someone in to do something, though. Couldn't you?'

'I can clear up my own mess. I do, when I feel like it.'

'There's nothing wrong in employing a cleaner.'

He said firmly, 'No one is going to get down on their hands and knees for me.'

'No one does, nowadays. They use mops with long handles, and electric cleaners.'

I thought: This is the first time we've been alone together for years and years and all I can talk about is housework. I started to laugh.

Steve said, 'That's better. You looked so scared, darling. As if you'd walked into a lion's den. Or a thieves' kitchen. Well, it is that, sometimes. Does Eddie know you're here?'

'He's in America. They've brought out a new edition of the novel and they're tying it in with the television series. He's doing a promotion tour. A coast-to-coast thing. He's hating it.'

Steve nodded. 'Oh. Good.' He frowned. 'I mean, I'm *sorry*. Of course. If he's not enjoying it. But it's good about the new edition. I hope it does well. How are the children?'

'Fine.'

'Good.'

'How are you?'

'Fine.' He ran his fingers through his hair and smiled at me. I said, 'How's Lolly?'

'She's taken her mother to Italy. For some sort of mud cure. They bury you up to your neck in mud. Lolly's mother has arthritis.'

'I'm sorry.'

'It keeps Lolly tied to her.'

'Oh.'

'So it's not altogether a disadvantage. From her point of view.'

'I see.'

'No, you don't. I don't mean it's an advantage for Lolly's mother. I mean it's useful for Lolly. It's less cramping being tied to a mother than being tied to a husband.'

He didn't sound bitter. I said, 'Do you want to marry her?'

'I don't know. Perhaps. It's not a question I ask myself often. Probably because I don't think she'd have me.'

I was ashamed. I said quickly, 'I'm sorry. I shouldn't have asked you. I don't know why I did. It's none of my business.'

'Oh, darling, please don't be silly.'

I put the blue-and-white mug down on the floor and balanced the half-eaten sandwich on top of it. I felt unbearably humiliated suddenly. I said, 'Please don't call me "darling".'

He stared at me. He looked very young still. A young man's soft, surprised face. I thought: It must be semi-starvation and all that fresh air on his motor bike. Or perhaps unmarried people always look younger. He said, 'Why on earth shouldn't I? I mean, I always have, haven't I?'

'That's the trouble. After you stopped loving me, you went on as if nothing had changed. I never could bear it. It seems so horribly cruel. Calling me "darling"! As if it meant nothing.'

'I never stopped loving you.'

I screwed my face up and gasped. Trying to get enough air to laugh.

He said, 'Please don't cry.'

'I'm not crying.' I turned my head away and looked at a calendar hanging on the wall next to the fireplace. It was last year's and showed a view of the Hebrides. I said 'I came to see you to talk about being a magistrate. I don't know whether I should be. I don't know if I'm a suitable person. No, that's not true. I mean, it's not only why I came. It was an excuse. I wanted to see you and I thought – well, it was a way of seeing you alone for once. Oh, that's not true, either. Nothing is simple. Coming here was an impulse. I don't know where it came from.'

'Poor Pen. I'm sorry.'

'Don't be sorry for me.'

'Are you very unhappy?'

'Of course not. Why should I be?'

'I can't tell you that, can I?'

I heard him sigh and the creak of old springs as he heaved himself out of his sagging chair. He was standing beside me, but I refused to look up at him. I stared sullenly, through blurred eyes, at the idyllic scene of a mountain glen on the calendar. He said, 'I hate to see you so miserable, dear. I don't know what to do. What to say. I suppose I may call you "dear"?' He laughed awkwardly.

'I'm not miserable, damn you.' Tears were running down my face; I couldn't stop them. I thought: As if a washer had gone on a tap. I was drowning in my own tears; drowning in a dark pit of sorrow. Bleeding internally. My life, my active, happy, purposeful life suddenly seemed empty to me, dreary and useless. The speed with which this had happened was terrifying. One minute I was walking calmly along, feet on firm ground, the next I had tumbled into this frightening, black chasm. How had it happened? Why did I feel like this? It was more than unhappiness. I had been unhappy occasionally, but I had always been able to pin down the cause. My marriage wasn't perfect, but whose marriage was? If I didn't love my children as much as I loved April's child, no one knew it but me, and I had done for my girls everything it was in my power to do. No one could do more, could they? I had thought I'd done well, been proud of the way I had learned to adjust, to compensate for the things that were lacking. Not that much was. I didn't want much for myself, only for others. And yet here I sat, weeping. . . .'

I said angrily, 'I've nothing to be miserable about. I mean, damn it *all*. I'm not sick, or starving, or poor. Roof over my head, shoes on my feet, husband and children. Spoiled, silly rich woman. Oh, I despise myself.'

'Never do that,' he said in a shocked voice, He knelt by the chair and put his arms round me. I leaned weakly against him while he stroked my hair, and began to feel better. Tears had healed the mysterious wound that had caused them in the first place. I said, 'I really don't know what made me cry.'

He giggled oddly, and kissed me. 'I'm not going to marry Lolly, my darling.'

I pulled myself upright, or as upright as I could in that dreadful chair, and said crossly, 'Do you think *that* upset me? I'd be happy for you if you got married, Steve! Or I'd try to be. I can't bear to think of you being lonely. I feel so lonely myself, suddenly. It's a commonplace thing, I suppose. The sort of thing that happens in the middle of one's life. You rush along busily and then you start wondering why. It all seems so pointless. I'm nearly *forty*, that's why I was crying. Nothing to do with you. Unless it's the bloody awful mess you are living in. Really, Steve, this place *smells*. How can you bear it?'

I said to Adam, last autumn, 'The truth is, I only became a magistrate because your Uncle Steve talked me into it.' And, remembering the circumstances in which he had done so, smiled inwardly. How shocked Adam would be if I told him we had discussed this solemn matter in bed! His aunt and his uncle, those two conscientious, trustworthy, high-minded, middle-aged people! Too old for sex from his point of view, perhaps? At our age, we should have given up that sort of thing, be devoting what remained of our elderly lives to good works and the stern contemplation of our latter end. Even if Adam didn't find the notion too displeasing aesthetically, he might well find it distasteful morally. I had been pontificating away about *his* misdeeds, telling him how to run *his* life better! No good trying to answer that life wasn't all of a piece, that, even if I misbehaved in one sphere, I could still act in another with perfect propriety. He would just think: How hypocritical. His two-faced old auntie!

Not that I felt, at any point, either two-faced or immoral. After that first, blissful night, I did not see Steve for ten days. During that time I argued my case over and over, not in a long, windy, enjoyably agonised way, but honestly and soberly and carefully, and came to the conclusion that a discreetly conducted double life was the only honourable course open to me. I was married to Eddie. I considered myself 'married' to Steve. Loving him, I was not embarking on an affair in the ordinary way but continuing something that had always been right. Although it had not seemed wrong at the time, the only really wrong thing I had done was to marry Eddie. Deceiving him with Steve, I was simply expiating that innocently committed long-ago crime – and found, with heady amazement, that I felt cleaner for it. It was not just the ordinary rejuvenation that comes with newly found love and sexual contentment. I had, altogether, a sense of renewal, as if my life, which had been a muddy stream, was suddenly flowing brighter and clearer from a sparkling and healthy source. I felt energetic and powerful and good, able to carry the sins of the world on my strong, willing shoulders. The evasions that became necessary when Eddie returned from America, even the occasional lies, were small penances that I performed cheerfully for the benefit of every-one who depended upon me: my husband, my children, my lover.

Steve suffered much more than I did. He felt guilty about Eddie as a sensitive man would naturally do (and, knowing myself to be coarser-grained, I honoured him for it), but I was able to persuade him that our happiness was not just a selfish indulgence but a force for more general good. If we had not rediscovered each other, the blackness that had been growing within me (and had made me weep that night in his flat) would have dragged me down, and my family too, in the end. Happy and at peace with myself, I could take care of Eddie better, be more tolerant, nag him less. Louise and Jenny would benefit from a mother whose energies were not concentrated on them during their adolescence (that notoriously difficult time for mother–daughter relationships) and who did not feel jealous of their flowering promise because she was so satisfied herself, sexually. And, when Steve still seemed to feel pinpricks of conscience, I told him that he could comfort himself with the thought that he might improve the lot of some of his clients by going to bed with a magistrate! He laughed when I said this, but it seemed true to me. Being happy, I would be kinder, want to build up, not destroy; being guilty (as I would be in some people's eyes if not in my own) would make me more understanding.

Sitting in court this warm, spring afternoon, I decide there is nothing wrong with these arguments. Even if, early on, I may have carried them to nonsensical lengths (Steve once said that I made committing adultery seem a positive duty) that doesn't make them invalid. Of course I had to justify myself. I always need to feel 'in the right', and that is a weakness. But it is true (at least, I think it is true) that I have been a nicer, more useful, more com-petent woman these last several years, partly because I have behaved in a way that would not seem, if it were out in the open, entirely honest or honourable.

While Abel's 'counsel makes his winding-up speech to the jury, I formulate my own defence privately. I have taken nothing from Eddie that he really wanted, and I have supported Steve in a way it seemed to me that he quite desperately needed. Not just with my love. His ascetism is not a priggish pose. He genuinely believes it is wrong to think of his own comfort or happiness when there is so much sorrow and poverty round him. But he has not prevented me thinking for him. Although he has refused to leave his squalid flat, I have been able to see, without stepping outside the disciplined limits he sets for himself, that his life there is a good deal more pleasant. I have kept his larder well stocked, his tatty clothes mended, found him a woman to clean the flat twice a week. She is not very competent, but Steve doesn't mind that; and as she is an unmarried mother he can persuade himself he is right to employ her because she must have a job where she can take her small baby with her. I have managed to do these things without hurting Eddie – indeed, with his consent and approval. When he came back from America, I told him I had been to see Steve and was shocked by the dreadful conditions he lived in. 'I can't bear to see him living like that. I really do feel I should do something about it.' 'Why not?' Eddie said. 'You've time to spare, pettikins, haven't you?' Even Steve's neighbours accept my regular visits as natural. When I speak of him to them I call him 'my brother'. The very thing that kept us apart now makes it easier for us to be happy together.

And, of course, being a magistrate has been useful too, given us additional 'cover'. Manning the frail barricades society throws up to protect itself against the pathetic army of victims that seeks to attack it, I have served on committees, visited prisons, driven long distances to lecture to schools on penal reform, attended weekend seminars on the theory of crime and punishment, and these occasions have often provided a chance to spend whole nights with my lover. I have never felt this was wrong or deceitful. Steve's interest in this side of my life has helped me, as I told him it would. Although I am not as tender as he is (sometimes Steve's attitude towards his clients seems to me to verge on the sloppy), he has taught me to understand a defendant's plight better. Whatever the rights and wrongs of his case, by the time he has got into court he is already partly defenceless : waiting and worry will have beaten him down. The sight of a bench of sober, trustworthy citizens who have obviously never broken the law in their lives or, worse still, a judge in a wig will complete the unmanning process. What chance has he got? The routine of the court does not help him. One moment he is allowed to sit down, a man among equals, the next the court usher – perhaps a retired army sergeant – will bark out that he must stand when he speaks to the Bench, like a schoolboy before a headmaster. He is flustered and frightened. He has something to hide, or at least will have to give intimate information about his life that he would prefer his best friends not to know. He has forgotten his driving-licence, mislaid his handkerchief, his pen, or his spectacles; he doesn't know what to do with his hands. Humiliation constricts his facial muscles; he screws up his eyes; is terrified that he may smile inadvertently. He wants to keep his dignity, but the odds are against him. Even if he is innocent he will begin to feel guilty.

If he is lucky, his judges will be aware of this. They may even be sorry for him. But they are more used to his situation than he is and they have their own troubles, ulcers and family worries and overdrafts at the bank, and if a simple case drags on too long irritation and boredom may diminish their sympathies.

In Abel Binder's case, certainly, boredom is affecting the jury. Unless it is the warmth in the court that is making them sleepy. Although the plump lady in the fur-collared coat is wide awake now (refreshed, perhaps, by her long doze of the morning), several of them are yawning. Or stifling yawns, anyway. The man sitting next to the sexy young girl has stopped eyeing her and is covertly picking his nose. She is touching her hair, pert little face softened and dreaming. Of a new dress? A boy-friend? The Ape

Man is watching the shadow of a trapped, drowsy fly buzzing between the lowered blind and the glass of the window beyond which the sun is still shining. Only the middle-aged lady in the neat woollen dress is obviously alert. She made notes while Abel's counsel was talking and now she is listening intently to the Judge summing up. Not that he has anything new to say. There is little he can add to what he said earlier, at the end of the morning. He repeats what he said then, speaking slowly and carefully about dishonest intention and its relevance in this particular case. I cannot help feeling that he could, if he wanted, make his point a little more eloquently. But presumably he does not wish to alienate the jury and appear to be usurping their function by instructing them too directly to acquit Abel Binder. It is comforting to feel sure that he knows what he is doing. I watch his profile, which is handsome if somewhat heavy, and imagine that strong, broken-veined nose, those full red lips, close to mine. I think: What an unsuitable moment for this kind of sexual fantasy. Of course, power is attractive, and the Judge is a powerful man. No doubt he has private failings but I do not know them and this is, I realise suddenly, why I find him attractive. It strikes me, with the force of a body blow, that I do not, in my heart, really care for weakness in others. I am astonished by this revelation; feel physically winded. My cherished view of myself as a tender, compassionate woman is a false view. The truth is, poverty and misfortune irritate me; the sight of people who cannot conduct their lives with at least a measure of competence makes me lose patience – as I have finally lost patience with Eddie's idleness, Eddie's tears. This is not why I am leaving him, but because I am leaving him I can admit it.

I really am leaving him! I can hardly believe it. I look at the clock as the Judge rises and think: How much longer?

It is half-past three. Waiting for the jury to reach their decision, I sit with the Judge and Goggle Eyes in a small, book-lined room, drinking the tea the usher has brought us. Only the Judge eats the sugary biscuits that are also provided. Goggle Eyes smokes a small, thin, black cigar with an unpleasant smell. I look at a bowl of spring flowers on the desk and wonder if they are a relic from the days when judges carried a posy into the court to ward off plague vapours. No one is talking, and I am free to let my mind wander. It is wonderfully invigorating to think that I may really be a quite different woman from the one I have imagined myself to be all these years. Like looking into a mirror and seeing a new and more interesting face looking out. Not a benevolent, uncomplaining bearer of burdens but a tougher, more ruthless and demanding spirit. One that has always been there, using the Penelope shown to the world as a front, a disguise. This is not an original idea, of course, nor so simple. Each human being contains within himself a whole cast of characters, a chorus of dissonant voices. Usually, for convenience, we select one main part to play; we need to be consistent in order to know who we are. And I have performed really quite creditably. I have discharged my duties as Eddie's wife, as Steve's mistress, as a mother, a magistrate – a moral juggler, craftily keeping all my balls in the air. It hasn't always been easy – there have been practical conflicts like the winter Eddie and Steve were both in bed with a chest infection at the same time; but my chosen role as a good woman, my proud sense of doing my best in difficult circumstances for everyone who depended on me, has made it possible. Now, suddenly, the self *I* have always depended upon has begun to look like a stranger, and, although this is exciting, it is also alarming. I am uncertain how this new Penelope will behave, how she *should* behave in this new situation that faces her. The uncertainty seems to be making me sweat. I sigh and touch the back of my hand to my brow.

The Judge says, 'Warm in here, isn't it? This building is always too hot or too cold. Shall I open the window?'

I shake my head, smiling at his bright, solicitous look. 'They won't be much longer, surely? The jury.'

Goggle Eyes shoots out his arm in a brisk salute and looks at his watch. He strokes the short, stiff hairs on his upper lip with a tobacco-stained finger. 'Over half an hour. Trouble is, I meant to look in at the office on my way home.'

'I hope we'll finish today,' the Judge says. 'I'm in another court tomorrow and I believe they have a full list. We don't want to run over. It might save time if we considered what to do with this man if the jury should find him guilty. I didn't think that was likely, but now they've been out so long I'm beginning to wonder.'

I say, 'An absolute discharge.' I do not believe it will come to this but I made up my mind some time ago and speak promptly.

The Judge takes the last biscuit. Specks of silvery sugar stick to his lips as he munches away. 'On the face of it, I'm inclined to agree with you. One assumes he's not been convicted before since the defence put in his good character as part of their evidence. But he may ask for other offences to be taken into consideration in which case an absolute discharge might not be proper, however lenient a view we take of this one.'

'But you do think he's innocent, don't you?'

'Oh, yes. I think we all do.' The Judge looks enquiringly at Goggle Eyes, who stubs out his vile cigar and nods gravely. He is not the sort of man to disagree with a judge, though he is probably argumentative on his own Bench with his fellow lay magistrates – particularly if they are female. His attitude towards women, I guess, is a mixture of furtive lust and contempt; they will hardly be, to his mind, worth taking notice of as rational beings. The Judge says, 'It's not our view that counts, though.'

'Unfortunately.' I smile at him, and the man under the slightly crooked wig smiles back at me cheerfully.

'Hundred pounds fine,' Goggle Eyes says. 'And costs, of course.'

I stare at him. The costs of a day's trial are quite beyond Abel's pocket! I say, 'Oh, come now, come off it!' realising that this outraged response will simply confirm this horrible man in his insufferable opinions about unstable, emotional women. 'He can't afford anything like that. The fine by itself is excessive for a man who is trying to keep a wife and two kids on his sort of income. And to add costs on too – well, I think that's unreasonable.'

Goggle Eyes bares his teeth. I have the impression that he would like to bite me. 'He knew what he was in for when he chose to be tried in this court. He's represented. He will have been told he will have to pay up if he's found guilty. I don't see, personally, why he shouldn't be made to. There's too much softness, too much take, take, take, in our present society. A man should stand on his own feet and be prepared to pay for his own mistakes, in my view.'

I long to shout abuse at him. 'In my view, you are a pure moral idiot.' Instead I say, in my stiffest, grand-lady manner, 'I think, in this case, that a fine of that order is really quite out of the question.'

The Judge says, 'It could hardly be less. But there are other ways of dealing with him if the jury find him guilty and there are other offences of perhaps a similar nature. Would you consider, say, a suspended sentence of six months and no costs?'

I don't like this, either. Although I was relieved when Adam was given a suspended sentence last autumn, I have been anxious since, thinking of the threat hanging over him. Does he take it seriously? Does he really understand that if he should be picked up again for possessing cannabis he will go to prison? I think: Adam and Abel! How biblical!

The Judge says, 'In effect, it will cause him less hardship. As long as he doesn't get into any more trouble.'

He is watching me gravely. His grave, courteous manner comforts and calms me, reminds me that this is, after all, merely an academic discussion; we all believe Abel is innocent. . . .

I say, 'Why do you think the jury are being so long?' I include Goggle Eyes in my question, smiling at him to show I am sorry for losing my temper. He doesn't smile back. His eyes make white,

angry circles around me. He said, 'I dare say they're finding something to argue about. Like the awkward little fact that he did
dispose of that car.'

An awkward, incontrovertible, intolerable *fact*. When I was first
aware of it, I was sure I must be mistaken. I had got the dates
wrong. I had been busy lately. This aspect of my life was so
automatic and unimportant now that I had dealt with it almost
unconsciously. For a little while – several days – these explanations
kept my mind quiet. Anything else was so unthinkable that I
couldn't think it! When I knew that I had to, I resolved to keep
calm. Ignore this one incident – I was getting older; it was not
impossible that I might start missing the occasional period – and
see what happened next month. When the time came and passed,
I still couldn't believe it. This absurd, farcical *thing* couldn't happen
to me! I had managed so well for so long; had sorted everything
out, everyone's needs, my own conscience. I had told myself: This
is what civilisation rests on. Honest people doing their best in
difficult circumstances. I had done my best, as I saw it, to weave
the different strands of my life into a harmonious, if intricate,
whole. Now this new fact has ruined the pattern. It cannot be
argued away, reasoned with. It makes all my cunning and skill,
all my finely tuned judgements, seem worthless. As if, all along,
I have been playing a game.

I didn't understand this immediately. I went to my doctor and
arranged for a pregnancy test. This was six days ago. I had been
nervous when I made the appointment; but sitting in the doctor's
surgery, chatting to him while he filled in the form for me to take
to the hospital, I felt suddenly cheerful, almost euphoric, like a
defendant whose case has been put off to be heard at a later date.
Although he knows that the reckoning will come, that he cannot
escape it, for the moment he feels as free as a bird. I actually drove
to the hospital singing! It was not until I had left the form and
the bottle of urine at the laboratory and was walking back to the

car-park that I realised something final had happened. Not *would* happen, in a few days, but *had* happened already. To go on pretending was childish. There must be no more childish games! I must make up my mind. Either to stay with Eddie, or to leave him for good. If I decided to stay, I must tell him at once that I might be having Steve's baby. To wait, to hang on until I was sure one way or the other, would be unspeakably sordid. A sordid admission that the way I had been running my life, a way I had believed to be good and beautiful because it made us all happy, had in fact been ugly and wrong from the beginning. The right course, the *only* course, if I were to hold my head high, have any respect for myself as a free moral agent, was to make my decision before it was forced upon me.

As I have done. I will know the result of the test later this afternoon. When the court rises, I will drive to the surgery, then to the railway station. I will leave the car in the park for Eddie to collect later (*his* car, after all, as are all our possessions) and take the train. Steve will meet me at his suburban halt halfway between here and London. He doesn't yet know what has prompted me to leave Eddie after all these years of calmly managed deceit because I have been too ashamed to tell him. Telling myself that it seems too undignified that the course of anyone's life should be altered by a flow of blood – or lack of flow – every month. Particularly my life, at my age! A moonstruck, middle-aged woman! But the cause of my shame lies deeper than this mildly silly embarrassment. I have always found my biological function humiliating, felt soiled and degraded, and knowing why has not helped me. Like that dreadful woman I was made to call 'Auntie', I cannot talk easily about 'that sort of thing'.

I think: Am I really leaving my husband because once, long ago, a scared little girl was driven to bury her bloody sanitary towels in a snow-covered cemetery? Oh, of course not. That little girl is still part of me, as are all those other Penelopes I have remembered today, but none of them are responsible for what I am doing.

Only a very soft-hearted judge would consider them credible as defence witnesses. I think: All these scenes from the life of a good woman! What do they amount to? Excuses, protestations of innocence, mitigating circumstances – all of them useless. It is actions that count in the end. What we are judged on.

The jury have reached their decision. The Ape Man delivers it. These twelve solid citizens have found Abel guilty of stealing that ancient Mercedes. They are all agreed on their unjust and unreasonable verdict, but since they have been out for an hour there must have been argument. The Intelligent Lady is sitting, mouth pursed, hands folded in the lap of her tan-coloured wool dress, eyes fixed coldly on distance. I like to imagine she has fought hard for Abel and lost but she may simply be thinking of her long journey home, the lonely meal she will eat while she watches television this evening, her old mother's terminal illness, or simply the state of the nation.

There are no emotional outbursts, no cries of protest. Abel stands woodenly while copies of his antecedents are handed up to the Bench. He has never appeared in a court before, being a man, as they say, of 'previous good character' – a description that has a forlorn ring now it no longer applies to him – but there is a list attached, as the Judge suspected there might be, of other offences he has not been charged with today but wants us to take into consideration before we pass sentence. None of these are remarkable, nor much of a threat to society. Indeed, to anyone concerned with the environment, Abel might seem an admirable scavenger, tidying up, not stealing, as he collected a few useful spare parts from the council tip to mend his old motor cars. Who else would have made such excellent use of the fuel pump, the alternator, the brake shoe, the clutch disc and the instrument cluster, which are among the items he has admitted to taking? Provident Abel has, in his small way, fought the good fight against urban pollution; industriously gleaning the scrapyards and recycling these bits of abandoned hardware, he has done his humble bit in the war against waste!

Unfortunately, this is not how the law looks upon his activities. Nor even, presumably, how Abel regards them. He has admitted his guilt in these matters before us and to argue, on his behalf, that he did not understand what he was doing would be to deny him his dignity. He has little else to console him. His counsel, on his feet, long red nose quivering, is speaking of his client's financial position which is, as I guessed it would be, too precariously balanced on the edge of real poverty to make a large fine a possible punishment. On the Bench, the Judge turns to Goggle Eyes, then to me. Abel watches us mutter together. I think: What do we look like to him? Three fallible people, mirror-images of his own human weakness? Or three cold, powerful enemies? Does he fear us? Or hate us? When Adam was standing his trial I sat in the public gallery, pain knotting my stomach, and watched the magistrates' faces for some sign of sympathy with my poor boy's predicament, but all I saw were three masks with nothing behind them. Remembering that anguished occasion I sigh and frown, deep thoughtful furrows lining my forehead, and hope that Abel will see my concern and be comforted. It is all I can do for him. I would still like to give him a discharge – whispering to the Judge that in my opinion his other offences are really too trivial to warrant a different decision – but he and Goggle Eyes are united against me. This is not a masculine conspiracy. I know before the Judge answers me that I am not being judicial. I want a discharge for Abel because that is what I want for myself. There is no connection between us, only this superstitious ache in my mind. If he goes free, so do I! I think: No one is rational. We are all guilty of something. Sometimes we need to punish an innocent man, as a scapegoat.

I say to the Judge, 'Six months, then. Suspended for one year.'

It is all over now. The court has risen. Goggle Eyes has scuttled off, full of importance: if he hurries, he will have time to 'look in at the office'. I imagine he will bully his secretary. I wonder if I should share this thought with the Judge but decide he might think it improper. We are standing outside his room. He shakes my hand warmly and thanks me for my help today. He says, 'I know you're unhappy about the way things turned out. Don't brood over it. Nor over that anonymous letter. Unless anything else untoward happens.'

'No.'

'It could have been a mistake, you know. Your name on an envelope for some other reason. An advertising pamphlet from some mailing-house. One of the office staff, a typist, perhaps, using it to give another girl a few aspirins. Then it got caught up in the delivery system.'

Has he been thinking this out all the time we were sitting in court? I say, 'I suppose that could happen.'

He smiles down at me, his full mouth moist as a fruit. 'If you're ever in London, why not give me a ring? We could have lunch together.'

Or dinner in his flat in the Albany? Music and candlelight; a prelude to seduction. I smile back and say, 'Thank you. I'd like that.'

I walk away down the corridor into the large central hall. It was crowded when I came through this morning; now only a few defendants remain, talking in hushed groups with their relations and lawyers. My feet make a sharp, clopping sound on the black and white tiles. I think: Like a trotting horse. Abel is standing alone, looking up at one of the portraits that line the dark walls. His hands in his pockets, a defeated droop to his shoulders. I will have to pass by this dejected figure. March straight past with my chin up. As I approach him, he turns; his eyes meet mine and I say, on impulse, 'I'm sorry.'

Close to, he looks older and coarser; his rosy skin scaly. He stares at me with unseeing, blue eyes. Does he recognise me? I am horrified, suddenly. I shouldn't have spoken to him. Will he spit in my face?

He shrugs his shoulders. One corner of his mouth lifts in an awkward half-smile. He is as embarrassed as I am by this encounter. I say boldly, 'It's no help, of course. I just wanted to say it. You must be feeling very fed up.'

'Can't be helped, can it?' He hesitates, then fumbles a pack of cigarettes out of his pocket and offers it to me. I take the first cigarette of my life and narrow my eyes against the smoke as he lights it. His solid hand, holding the match, trembles slightly.

I inhale and gasp. I say, coughing, 'You could appeal, of course. Though I can't advise you. You should ask your solicitor.' Steve would make him appeal! There are grounds. The jury wilfully ignored the Judge's direction. I think: How outraged Steve will be when I tell him. He has a quotation from Tolstoy painted on his bathroom wall so that he will see it when he shaves every morning. *Human law. What a farce!*

Abel shakes his head. 'It's best left. I've done with solicitors now.' He lights his own cigarette and seems more at ease with this cancerous tube between his strong. stubby fingers. 'If I'd had my way I'd have got it finished with in the magistrate's court. I meant to plead guilty. Trouble was, when I went there and told them what happened, they said to change my plea and get legal aid. And the solicitor said, go to the Crown Court. you'll have more luck with a jury.' He smiles openly now; his nice smile. 'Seems he was wrong.'

'You were unlucky. Things don't always work out as they should. It could have gone the other way, easily.'

'I just wish I hadn't let it drag on. There's been all this long time, and the worry. My wife's upset; her mother gets at her all the time, and she's under the doctor for nerves. Now there's this sentence. I don't know how she'll take it.'

I say, 'I really am sorry.'

'That's nice of you. It makes me feel better.' This is not intended ironically. He adds, 'I mean, you heard it all, so you know.'

'There's no justice, really.' I laugh as I say this standing in this chilly, badly lit hall with dead judges frowning down at me from their heavy-framed portraits. I don't want him to take me too seriously.

'Oh, I wouldn't say that. It was a fair enough trial, wasn't it? Everyone listened. I'm not complaining. I sat there and thought: Well, you could look at it two ways. . . .' He looks at me hesitantly and gives a little, uneasy cough, politely lifting the back of his hand to his mouth. 'I mean, I've been lifting odd bits off the dumps quite a while. Several years. I never thought nothing of it. They was just a few old spares no one else had any use for. I knew it was against the law but I thought: That's something different. It wasn't, though, was it? It was stealing, really. It's being caught bringing it home.'

'Yes. Yes, I know.'

I drop my half-smoked cigarette on the tiled floor and grind it out with my shoe. It wasn't as unpleasant as I had expected, but I feel slightly giddy. I look at my watch – the gold watch Eddie gave me on my fortieth birthday – and know I ought to go now. But it seems discourteous to leave too abruptly.

I say, 'Well, it's over now. You can forget all about it. Put it behind you.'

I am aware this sounds patronising. But I don't know what to say to him any more than he knows what to say to me. We smile at each other uncomfortably.

He says, suddenly, 'You were on my side, weren't you? That's what it looked like to me.'

I say, 'Well. . . .' I shouldn't be holding this conversation. Magistrates should never discuss a case with a defendant. I stiffen my face and lower my eyelids like shutters.

Abel says, 'I didn't trust that other bloke, though. Old Frog Face.' He looks at me closely. 'Sorry. I oughtn't to say things like that. It's not fair.'

'It doesn't matter.'

'Looks a bit funny, though, us talking like this. If anyone notices. I don't want to get you into trouble.'

I shake my head, laughing. 'I have to go now, anyway. So will you. They'll be shutting this place up in a minute.'

The hall is almost empty. The ushers are waiting to turn the lights off. The Judge will have gone by now, leaving by a side exit. I could have left that way too; avoided this meeting with Abel.

I start walking and he walks beside me, along a carpeted corridor, down a flight of shallow, carpeted stairs. I say, 'Do you want a lift anywhere? My car's outside.'

'I've got my bike.'

He opens the door for me. It swings shut behind us. The spring warmth has gone from the air, which has a blue tinge to it. In the regimented flower-beds, the tulips are tightening their petals.

I take my keys out of my bag. We stand by my car. I am waiting for Abel to go, but he seems too heavy and weary to move, as if his limbs are weighed down and weakened by exhaustion and disappointment. Everything has hung on this day; now it is over and his whole life has crumbled. He has to go home and face his family; his wife's nagging mother. How can he bear it?

I think: I can help him. Helping people is one thing I know I am good at. I say, 'Look, I know it's none of my business, really. But I do understand how you feel. I mean, I know how this sort of thing affects people. Although it seems awful now, almost unbearable, it won't seem quite so awful tomorrow. And by next week it will have begun to fade so you will only think of it sometimes. In the end, you'll just remember it as a silly mess you got into once. Things seem terribly important at the time, enormous great mountains you can never climb, but after a while they become part of the landscape. What you see when you look back. Of course you have to get through today. Tell your wife – I can see that's the worst part. The whole family waiting at home. If I were you, I wouldn't go back immediately. Ring your wife first. Ask her to meet you somewhere – at the pub, perhaps, after she's put the children to bed. Buy her a drink and tell her what's happened, talk it over quietly, then go home and tell her parents. It will be easier that way. The two of you together.'

I unlock the car door and get into the driving-seat. I look up at Abel and he looks down at me. He says. 'We're not on the phone. But thanks all the same.'

His solid face is alight with amusement. He beams at me with kindly affection, then says – changing the subject to make me feel less of a fool? – 'Nice job, this car, isn't it? Has it got fuel injection?'

'Yes.'

'Had any trouble with it?'

'A bit, in the beginning. It let us down once or twice when it got over-heated. Something electrical.'

He nods, standing back and regarding the bodywork like a sales-man looking for scratches. He says, 'Half a tick.' He bends to touch the ground by the front wheel, sniffs at his forefinger. He prods it towards me and I smell rancid almonds.

I say, 'What is it?'

'Brake fluid. Hang on.'

He kneels on the ground in his good suit and twists his head under the car, round the back of the wheel. I can see the red, shaved back of his neck above his tight shirt-collar.

I say 'Please don't bother. You'll get your clothes dirty.'

He grunts something; then crouches back on his haunches. He tugs his handkerchief out of his pocket as he stands up; wipes his hands. 'You've got trouble there, I'm afraid. The fluid's drained out. Pretty near all of it.' He is looking embarrassed and puzzled.

I say, 'It was all right this morning. I drove here quite safely.'

'Well, you could have done. It depends on how fast it's been leaking. But I reckon if you was to set off now, and put your foot on the brake, you'd just sail straight on.'

I feel cold. Veins running icy water; legs and arms tingling. I say, 'What can have happened?'

'There's a screw undone. You can see the clean thread. Could have worked loose, but I doubt it. More likely, someone didn't screw it up properly. Unless they unscrewed it on purpose.' He laughs loudly at this absurd suggestion.

I laugh with him. 'How long does it actually take to drain out the brake system?'

'As I said, it depends. I'd need to fill up and test with the screw open in this position. At a guess, I'd say it had been done fairly recently. Within the last twenty-four hours, anyway.'

'Or *not* done!' I cry, laughing with fearful, forced gaiety. 'The thing *is* I had this wretched car serviced yesterday. I always knew our garage was pretty incompetent!'

I am too shocked to feel anything. All I can do is laugh like a braying donkey and lie. I think: Who am I defending?

He looks apologetic. 'I don't know. You'd have noticed, now, wouldn't you? You'd have tried the brakes, backing out.'

'Yes. Yes, of course. Thank you, anyway.'

'Don't mention it,' Abel says, smiling.

Sitting in the train half an hour later, I think: I might be dead now. Crashed into the back of a truck, thrown through the windscreen, my face cut to pieces, neck broken. Or have killed someone else; mown down some running child or an old woman on a pedestrian crossing. Did Eddie think of that possibility? If it was Eddie. Who else, though? The car has not been to the garage for months. Eddie is not mechanically minded in general – it is always I who mend fuses, fix dripping taps, change his typewriter ribbons – but he would know how to immobilise vehicles. One of the tricks of wartime resistance. How to write off your enemy! Why should Eddie want to do this to me? Why should *anyone*? Was it just meant as a message; a sign, like those aspirins? 'You tiresome bitch, this is what we all think of you.' I cannot believe it. I have tried so hard always.

The railway runs along the side of the hill. Briefly, before it turns into the cutting, I can look down upon the place I am leaving. From this vantage-point, the motorway appears less intrusive, its elegant curves shaped and confined by the gentle slopes of the valley. Like the calm, silver lakes of the gravel pits that the residents of Cedar Grove once objected to just as violently, the new road is settling in, becoming part of the landscape. Dusk, of course, softens everything. In this pearly grey haze, even the hideous Gothic asylum, towers and turrets twinkling with fairy lights, has the enchantment of a fairy-tale castle. I think: Poor Eddie, what a fate! To be accused by *two* wives of attempted murder! But I am not mad, like Estelle. I know this is fantasy. Oh, the *facts* may be real, the aspirins, the brakes (unless Abel was mistaken, or lying – frightening me, perhaps, to get his own back?), but it is my guilty mind that has given them this monstrous significance.

I shall never know the truth now. I have left the car at the court; left the keys with the office, warning them not to let any-one drive it until the brakes have been seen to. That was all I had time for; I had made myself late, talking to Abel. I took a taxi to the surgery, picked up the note from my doctor, and caught this train by the skin of my teeth, running across the bridge lugging my heavy suitcase. Now I am sitting in a first-class, non-smoker's compartment, looking out at the scenery (my transparent reflection superimposed upon it like a ghostly photograph) and holding my doctor's letter crumpled up in my hand. A piece of paper. My passport to freedom.

I have not thought about being free before. I was so sure I must be pregnant and, as the days passed, the certainty grew. When Abel said, 'being caught brings it home,' I echoed him silently. Adultery is theft, people say, and although, in my special case, I can hardly be accused of stealing from Eddie I have short-changed Steve for a long time. I have had several people to love; he has only had me. The life we have has suited my energetic, ebullient temperament – all that rushing about, the planning, even the secrecy – but perhaps Steve has sometimes regarded it differently. I can't remember the last time I asked him if he was happy.

There are so many unasked, and unanswered, questions. And so many things I can do, now I am free to choose. I could go back to Eddie. All that I said in the letter I tucked into his typewriter was that I had decided to leave him and that I was sorry; if I were to return now, he would weep with joy and forgive me. Or I could live with Steve. Not in that flat, that would be *unendurable,* but in some pleasant, small house, humble enough to suit his thrifty nature, and comfortable enough for mine. I realise, with a slight shock – as if I had hailed an old friend from a distance, and found closer to, that she was a stranger – that both these prospects strike me as boring. . . .

I say aloud, 'Ho, hum!' and laugh idiotically at my face in the window. There is, of course, another alternative. I could start afresh. Forget the past, throw off the old shackles, live for myself for a change! I have enough money. Eddie settled thirty thousand pounds on me when we got married. I wouldn't dream of taking an income from him (except to begin with, perhaps, before I have found some way of earning my living), but he would be deeply wounded if I tried to hand him his wedding-gift back. I will use it to buy a house or a flat with enough room for the girls to come and stay when they want to. We will have a better relationship once we are free, working women together not mother and daughters. I shall have a job, as they will. And I will continue with my work as a magistrate. I shall resign from my local people and apply to the Lord Chancellor for an appointment in Inner London. I shall meet new people. Entertain! I might even ring up the Judge and invite him to dinner!

I smile at this thought and my reflection grins back at me wickedly. I speak sternly to it. 'My good woman, are you out of your mind? This isn't like you!' I lift my chin, frowning slightly, and find this grave, mature look rather more recognisable. I am not really frivolous. It is just that I have had a series of shocks today and they have shattered me more than I realised. I feel blown apart; splintered. I tell myself I am tired, that is all. If I hang on, through this time of confusion, the pieces will come together and make sense again. Steve loves me and needs me – I must hang on to *that*! He has been patient and generous so long. If it had not been for me, he might have married, had children. There will be no child now, but I can make this lack up in other ways and perhaps, at our age, to be childless is better. I can give him my undivided love and attention.

The train draws into the suburban station. There are not many people about at this time of the evening; a few wives going to London, to the theatre, or to dine with their husbands; a few rail-way employees going home at the end of their shift. Steve is standing close to the barrier. He is wearing an old navy raincoat and a trailing, striped scarf, one end of which sweeps the ground. A casual observer might think him a schoolboy, but although his eyes search the train he is not boyishly agitated, and the light under which he is standing shines down on the composed and civilised face of a man who is accustomed to waiting. Penelope sits, holding her breath, watching him with the strained excitement of a criminal eyeing a policeman. A whistle blows; doors slam hollowly. Pene-lope has a moment of panic – but, after all, if she changes her mind, she can always say she fell asleep on the train. And a moment of guilt – but, again, if Steve really wants her, he can always come after her. Then, as the train jerks into uneven motion, the oddest thought of all comes to her. It is not she who is evading her duties and obligations, but Steve who has had a lucky escape! This strange, disconcerting idea, appearing almost subliminally on the busy screen of her mind, has vanished before her carriage reaches the end of the platform. She settles comfortably into her seat and while the train gathers speed begins to compose in her mind a letter to the Lord Chancellor.